IT TAKES TWO

A Lot to Tackle

by Belle Payton

Simon Spotlight

New York   London   Toronto   Sydney   New Delhi

SIMON SPOTLIGHT
An imprint of Simon & Schuster Children's Publishing Division
1230 Avenue of the Americas, New York, New York 10020
This Simon Spotlight edition September 2015
Text by Heather Alexander
Cover art by Anthony VanArsdale
© 2015 by Simon & Schuster, Inc.
All rights reserved, including the right of reproduction in whole or in part in any form.
SIMON SPOTLIGHT and colophon are registered trademarks of Simon & Schuster, Inc.
For information about special discounts for bulk purchases, please contact Simon & Schuster Special Sales at 1-866-506-1949 or business@simonandschuster.com.
Designed by Ciara Gay
The text of this book was set in Garamond.
Manufactured in the United States of America 0815 OFF
10 9 8 7 6 5 4 3 2 1
ISBN 978-1-4814-4203-9 (hc)
ISBN 978-1-4814-4202-2 (pbk)
ISBN 978-1-4814-4204-6 (eBook)

Library of Congress Control Number 2014952441

CHAPTER ONE

"State! State! State!" The chant filled the crowded restaurant, echoing off the wood-beamed ceilings. Fans pounded the rhythm onto the worn tables. People just walking in immediately started stamping their feet to the beat in the aisles, dodging the waitresses balancing trays of steaming ribs and steaks.

Ava Sackett chanted so loudly that her throat hurt. The Ashland Tigers football team was going to the State Championships!

She felt dizzy with excitement. Everyone in town was celebrating tonight, but Ava was sure that she was the happiest of all. This past summer, her family had moved from Massachusetts to Ashland, Texas, just so her dad could coach the high school team to victory. A lot of people had doubted him—but not Ava. She'd known Coach would lead the team all the way to the play-offs. And she knew he would win State, too.

Ava watched her twin sister Alex weave her way back from the bathroom at Fighting Tiger BBQ through the mass of fans. Strangers called out their congratulations. Alex beamed as she slid onto the bench next to Ava.

"Perfume much?" Ava teased, holding her nose. As usual, her twin sister had overly spritzed herself with the honeysuckle body mist that she carried in her navy cross-body bag.

"You should try it," Alex teased back, knowing that unlike her, Ava refused to wear makeup and perfume. "Besides, I can't handle smelling like cooked cow."

"You don't have to put it that way!" Ava cried. Alex had become a vegetarian this year, so she wasn't a huge fan of the many barbecue restaurants in Texas.

Their older brother, Tommy, pushed in alongside Alex, squishing the twins closer together. Tommy had bulked up since he'd started playing high school football. The three of them barely fit onto the booth's bench.

The restaurant grew louder than other Friday night postgame celebrations. People roared, pretending to be actual tigers. Ava inhaled. Though she wasn't a fan of Alex's perfume, the familiar sweet floral scent comforted her in the chaos. She wasn't big on crowds.

"Austin, here we come," Alex said. She gazed across the table at their mom. "We're *all* going to the game, right? You and Daddy promised."

"Of course!" Coach jumped in. "I need my family with me in Austin."

The championship game would be played two weeks from that night at the big university stadium in the state capital. Austin was a few hours away, so they'd have to stay overnight in a hotel. Ava hoped it would be a nice one with room service.

"Alex and I will check out all the cute boutiques and art galleries." Mrs. Sackett clapped her hands together.

"For sure!" Alex agreed, twirling a strand of her long, chocolate-brown hair.

Shopping was one of Alex's passions, but it certainly wasn't one of Ava's. Dressing rooms held the top spot on her Most Hated Places list. Give her a worn jersey over a dress and tights any day! The Sackett twins looked identical, except for Alex's long hair and Ava's short hair, but when it came to their likes and dislikes, they were polar opposites.

"And there's this restaurant I'm dying to try called Mercury Grill. It's small and very fancy," Mrs. Sackett said.

"Is that the one we saw on TV?" Ava asked. She loved to watch cooking shows with her mom, even if she didn't love cooking itself.

"Exactly." Mrs. Sackett had a dreamy, faraway look in her eyes.

"Football first," Coach reminded her.

"Way to go, Sacketts!" Xander Browning waved a barbecued spare rib at them from across the room.

Ava waved back. Xander was also in seventh grade. He sat next to his older brother, who played defense on the high school team. After the game, most of their other friends had headed to Sal's, the small pizza place where the middle school kids hung out. But Mrs. Sackett had insisted that tonight was family night.

"This is crazy, right?" Alex called over the noise. "We're celebrities." Her green eyes sparkled. Alex loved the attention.

"Great job, Coach!" Floyd Whittaker cried. His enormous 1979 high school football ring gleamed as he slapped Coach on the back. He was a former Tigers player. "We crushed the Falcons."

Mr. Whittaker loudly reviewed the final run of PJ Kelly, the quarterback, with the group of former players crowded around the table. Coach nodded but said little. He stole glances at his phone, which rested on the table.

"Any word?" Mrs. Sackett said softly. She tilted her head toward the phone.

"Not yet." Coach glanced up and waved to another fan calling his name.

"What about you, Little Sackett? Going to get us the win tomorrow, too?" For a moment, Ava didn't realize that Mr. Whittaker was talking to her.

"Uh, sure. I hope so," Ava said.

"Got to have more confidence than that!" Mr. Whittaker boomed. "Got to keep up the Sackett tradition!"

Ava gulped. The middle school football team had their play-off game tomorrow. She played kicker and sometimes wide receiver. She was the only girl on the team, but that no longer seemed the big deal it'd been at the beginning of the season. Winning was the focus—even more so now that the high school team was heading to State.

"Ava's got it covered." Tommy reached across Alex and gave Ava a high five.

Coach picked up his phone to respond to a flurry of texts.

"How is he?" Mrs. Sackett finally asked.

"Who?" Mr. Kelly demanded, joining the conversation. Even though he wasn't on the coaching staff, PJ's dad liked to know everything about the team.

"Dion's going to be okay." Coach didn't look up, as his thumbs punched the keys.

Mrs. Sackett let out a relieved breath. Dion Bell, the second-string quarterback, had been tackled roughly in the fourth quarter. He'd walked off the field, but when he complained of dizziness after the game, his parents had driven him to the hospital. Most of the fans didn't know he'd been hurt.

The night's excitement drained from Coach's face. "But he does have a concussion. He's out for State."

"Out?" Tommy's usually deep voice erupted in a squeak.

"Out?" Mr. Whittaker boomed.

"Out?" Mr. Kelly echoed.

Coach nodded. "He can't risk being tackled again. It's the smart choice not to play."

Ava watched as all the men around their table moved their gaze to her brother. Tommy, who'd rarely made it off the bench this season as third-string quarterback, would take over Dion's spot. PJ Kelly would be first-string quarterback, but if something happened to him, Tommy would go in.

"You could play in State!" Ava cried, unable to hide her excitement.

"Boy, you just won the jackpot!" Mr. Kelly said. Ava nodded. Every boy in Texas dreamed of playing quarterback in the State Championship football game. A lot of girls probably did too. And Tommy might have the chance. How lucky was he?

Tommy pressed his lips together tightly and nodded. He looked nervous.

"Sacketts all the way!" Mr. Whittaker cried.

"Sackett! Sackett!" The restaurant erupted with chants of their last name.

Ava couldn't stop smiling. Coach and Tommy were part of Ashland football royalty! And at tomorrow's game, she'd kick the ball so far and so high that they'd chant for her, too.

Alex scanned her checklist on Saturday morning as the Ashland Middle School cheerleaders reached for corn muffins and breakfast burritos. Pitchers of orange juice stood next to a big pot of coffee, where the moms had gathered. Several stifled yawns and complained about the early hour.

Wimps, Alex thought. She'd been up since sunrise. There was so much to do before the big football game. She'd already set up the pregame breakfast for the cheerleaders at Rosa Navarro's house. And Alex wasn't even on the squad.

No surprise there, she thought. She'd never been able to touch her toes. Splits would surely send her to the hospital. And forget back handsprings!

Her best friends in Ashland, Lindsey Davis and Emily Campbell, were cheerleaders, so she'd tried out to be with them. What a joke! She'd happily ditched the pom-poms when she discovered that she could be in charge of the squad's public relations instead.

Wait! Pom-poms! Alex checked her list. "Excuse me!" she called over the noise. "Don't forget to pick up your new pom-poms in the box by the front door before the game. I ordered metallic silver ones for the play-off game. You guys will really sparkle!"

"Woo-hoo! Thanks, Alex!" Lindsey called. Several other girls cheered.

"And bows," Alex said, reaching into a bag by her side. "I bought silver hair bows too."

"Where did you get the money for all this?" Mrs. Navarro asked, shaking her head in amazement.

"Oh, you know, fund-raising. We had that bake sale two weeks ago. And I decorated jars with ribbons and placed them in all the stores in town for donations. We raised a lot of money that way," Alex said proudly. "Eat up, everyone! You'll need to leave for the field in thirty minutes."

Alex pulled a second piece of paper out from under her checklist. She had tallied all the cheerleaders who'd already paid for the coach's gift. Now she went from family to family to collect the remaining money. *I'll need to walk into town this week and buy something nice for Coach Jen,* she thought. But what? People who had no imagination bought candles and hand cream. She liked to give gifts that had meaning.

Maybe a pretty picture frame, she thought. *And I'll pose the squad for a photo to place in the frame. Excellent!*

"Before everyone leaves, we need to snap a photo!" she called. She added the photo to her list.

"Alex, you amaze me," Mrs. Campbell said, handing her five dollars for the coach's gift. She turned to Mrs. Navarro. "You watch. This girl is going places."

"I agree." Mrs. Navarro rested her hand on Alex's shoulder. "Alex has it all together. She's a superstar!"

Alex felt a blush blanket her pale cheeks, but she wasn't really embarrassed by the attention. She liked being a superstar!

"I predict that you'll run a huge company someday," Mrs. Navarro announced.

"Alex Sackett will be mayor of Ashland," Emily interjected.

"Oh, please!" Lindsey moved into the conversation. She hated not being the center of attention. "You have to think bigger. Alex will be president of the United States."

Emily nudged her. "Hey, Alex. Stop being so perfect. You're making the rest of us look bad." Emily grinned, and Alex knew that her friend was teasing.

"I'm so not perfect," she said.

Emily rolled her eyes. "Tell that to the teachers."

Mrs. Campbell nodded. "Emily tells me that not only are you helping the cheerleading squad, but you were elected seventh-grade class president and your grades are out of this world. All As!"

Alex shrugged modestly, secretly delighted by the shower of praise. She dreamed of being a senator or a governor someday. Or even running a big business with thousands of employees. Middle school was the beginning of bigger things. Much bigger.

And then her mind flashed back to the big red B scrawled at the top of her English quiz yesterday.

She chewed her lip. Her first B on a quiz, ever. She hadn't told her parents or Ava. Her mom and dad were too busy before the big football game to worry about her English grade, and telling Ava seemed unfair. Ava would be happy with a B. Thrilled, even. Alex tried to make a point of never bragging to her twin how easily school came to her. Ava struggled with ADHD, and that made focusing on schoolwork more difficult for her.

Alex sighed. She knew why she'd gotten that B. She'd been making posters for the playoff game and organizing this cheerleader breakfast. She hadn't had time to make her special color-coded study sheet.

No big deal, she told herself. *I'm a superstar. One B isn't going to mess that up.*

Alex excused herself and headed to the kitchen for a glass of water. On the way, she pulled out her phone and searched for the number of the restaurant in Austin her mom had mentioned last night. Before bed, she and Ava had decided to surprise her parents by making a reservation. What better way to celebrate after the championship game? Alex said she'd call, since Ava had to warm up before her own game.

Alex listened as the phone rang.

"Hello, you've reached Mercury Grill. We're closed right now. Please leave a message at the beep." The recording was delivered by a man with a deep voice.

Alex left her phone number and glanced at the time. Of course—fancy restaurants weren't open this early. She'd add calling them back to her list.

"Alex, hey, Alex!" Lindsey tugged at Alex's royal-blue sweater. "I need your opinion."

Alex looked up. Lindsey and Emily stood before her in their cheerleading uniforms and perfect blond ponytails.

"About what?" Alex asked. She self-consciously re-did the hair band on her own ponytail, smoothing down the flyaways.

"Me and Corey," Lindsey said. "Tomorrow is our two-month anniversary."

"Oh. Wow! Congrats," Alex said.

"I want to do something nice for him," Lindsey said.

"Something romantic," Emily added.

Alex wondered what *she* would do. Maybe share the huge Arctic Blast sundae at Rookie's or fly side by side on that new zip line at Adventureland. She gave a small chuckle. Who was she kidding? She'd never had a boyfriend for two hours, let alone two months.

When she'd first moved to Ashland, she'd actually wished Corey would be her boyfriend.

That was before she knew about his history with Lindsey—and before she and Lindsey became friends. Now the idea that he could have been into her seemed crazy! Everyone at school, including Alex, saw that Lindsey and Corey were so right together, even though it was kind of a cliché. He was the middle school quarterback. She was a cheerleader. Their mothers had been college roommates, linking Lindsey and Corey together since they were born.

"Alex, you keep spacing out on us." Lindsey's voice broke through her thoughts.

"Oh, sorry." Alex looked back at her phone. She'd have to remind the cheerleaders about their new pom-poms again. It was almost time to go.

"What about a party?" Lindsey asked. "An anniversary pizza party!"

"I love parties!" Emily clapped her hands together. "We can all celebrate with you."

"All of us?" Alex wrinkled her nose. "Isn't that . . . well, a lot?"

"It'll be fun," Emily insisted. "We can do it at my house tomorrow night. We can make it a surprise for Corey."

"He'll be shocked. We'll get all his friends

and our friends too. I'll be the most awesome girlfriend!" Lindsey bounced on her toes.

"Do you think he'll want that?" Alex asked. A pizza party didn't sound very romantic.

"Sure," Lindsey said confidently. "Will you help me plan it, Alex? You're so good at organizing these things."

"Well . . . I . . ." She liked parties, but something about Lindsey's idea felt wrong. For two months of going out, a party seemed a bit excessive.

Stop it, Alex chided herself. *Corey is Lindsey's boyfriend. She knows him best.*

"I'll totally help," Alex promised. She pulled out another piece of paper and began to make a party list.

CHAPTER TWO

"Shove over, Sackett." Ava looked up to see Corey O'Sullivan drop down beside her. He pulled off his helmet, pushing his dark-red hair from his eyes. Beads of sweat lined his forehead. "That was a disaster," he muttered.

Ava inched down the bench in the boys' locker room. The thirty boys around her had accepted that she was as much a part of this team as any of them. She struggled to breathe through the stench of mildew, sweat, and an overabundance of spray-on deodorant. Even though she didn't like perfume, she almost suggested they move their halftime meeting to the girls' locker room.

But today wasn't the time for cute remarks.

"We're down twenty-one to fourteen. We've been down before. And what do we do? We come back to win!" Coach Kenerson called out. "It's the final play-off game, and you guys looked nervous out there. You made too many mistakes. We need to relax. Each and every one of you needs to push himself"—he looked at Ava—"or herself to be better than you thought you could be. There's no other time but now. If we turn it around and win, we're on to the championships, just like the high school team last night."

Ava nodded. The entire first half of the game had been a mess, full of mistimed throws and missed catches. Nobody was in the groove. And the other team, the Plainview Pioneers, was playing a more aggressive game than any team they'd been up against all season.

"We can't let this slip away." Corey stood and addressed the team. "We've got to work together. We can do this!"

They formed a huddle. All hands dropped into the middle. "Go Tiger Cubs!" they cried, raising their hands high.

Ava joined in the cheer. She wanted this win for her dad, for the team, and for herself. She'd fought the school board for a place on the team.

Getting to the championships would prove not only that she belonged but that she was a vital player. As they walked back onto the field, she vowed to play better.

The second half began. Ava anxiously waited for the opportunity to kick.

"Go! Go!" she cried, as Corey bulleted the ball to wide receiver Owen Rooney. Owen, who was famous for his golden hands, misjudged the distance. The ball bounced onto the turf five feet behind him. The Pioneers snatched it for an interception.

"What's he doing?" Ava cried in frustration.

"He's having a bad day," Bryce Hobson said. Bryce was also a kicker, and he sat alongside her, helplessly watching the action. "Everyone is."

"We can't all have a bad day *today*!" Ava paced the sideline, unable to stay seated on the bench. She grimaced as Owen repeatedly got tackled on the next few passes.

Coach Kenerson stood with his arms crossed and his eyebrows knitted together in a disgruntled V. Ava had played wide receiver countless times in practice. She was sure she could catch the balls Owen had missed. Would Coach K put her in?

But the game moved into the fourth quarter,

and Owen stayed in his position. They managed to score another touchdown on a pass caught by Greg Fowler. Ava hated not being part of the action. *If only I could get a chance like Tommy has now that Dion is out,* she thought. She knew she shouldn't think this, but if Owen got sick or a little bit hurt, she could take the field and run for the touchdown they so badly needed. She was ready to be the hero.

Please, oh, please put me in so I can do something great, she thought.

But Coach Kenerson remained loyal to Owen.

"Go! Go!" Ava cheered as loudly as she could for Owen and Corey, hoping to encourage them to play as well as they had all season.

When the final twenty seconds of the game flashed on the scoreboard, the Ashland Tiger Cubs were down 24–23. Minutes earlier, they'd scored two points when Xander sacked the quarterback in the Pioneers' own end zone. Coach Kenerson called a time-out. He motioned Ava over.

"There's no way we're getting a touchdown." He locked eyes with her. "It's a long shot, I know. I'm not asking for miracles, but one field goal will do the trick."

Ava gulped and noted the field position. She'd

have to kick the ball from thirty-nine yards out. She'd never cleared the crossbar from that far away in a game. She rarely attempted that distance in practice.

She gazed at the Texas flag hanging limp on the pole by the concession stand. No wind today. That was good.

What could she say? She had to try. And besides, hadn't she wanted to go in and save the game? She couldn't believe that this impossible kick was how she was getting her wish.

She secured her helmet in place and jogged onto the field. The cheerleaders pumped up the crowd with a new routine. The bleachers erupted with a blur of noise, but she focused only on the goalposts looming in the distance.

Too far, she thought. Her stomach plummeted. How had the game come to this?

Suddenly the crowd's noise stopped sounding like noise, and she heard the chant: "Sackett! Sackett!"

They were chanting for her.

Her eyes searched the bleachers, landing on Coach's orange baseball cap. Her mother waved frantically next to him. Tommy pumped his fist. Alex stood down near the cheerleaders, who were all going crazy. Her stomach churning with nerves, she looked again at Coach. He met her gaze with a look of steely determination.

Ava inhaled deeply. She knew that look. He was right. She had a job to do. She had to kick this ball as far as she could. The snap came, and her foot connected solidly with the ball. She watched it arc into the sky.

Then Ava turned away.

She didn't need to watch what she already knew. The kick hadn't been far enough. The ball would fall short.

A second later, the referee's whistle blew, ending the game and the Tiger Cubs' season. The Pioneers exploded into a rallying cry as Ava fought back the tears that threatened to run rivers down her cheeks.

Do not cry. Do not cry, she repeated, as she walked slowly off the field.

"Tough one," Logan Medina said as she found her way back to the bench.

"Not your fault," Bryce added.

Many other boys chimed in, giving her consoling pats on the back.

Coach Kenerson gathered the players together, but Ava barely heard his words. She knew it wasn't her fault exactly. The whole team had played badly. The game shouldn't have come down to that long-distance kick. But she still felt responsible for the loss.

". . . you should be proud of your magnificent season," he finished. "Walk with your heads held high. Look how far you came as a team. Let's have a team cheer."

Thirty boys and Ava slung their arms around one another and let out the Tiger roar. In the deafening noise, Ava finally allowed herself a small smile. Being part of this team was one of the best things that had ever happened to her. One bad kick wouldn't take that away.

Next year will be even better, she told herself. She'd practice kicking longer and farther. Then nothing could stop them from making it to the championships.

CHAPTER THREE

"See? This is good. Right?" Alex stood on the top step of Emily's front porch. Through the nearby bay window, she spotted the profiles of Emily, Lindsey, Rosa, Annelise Mueller, and Charlotte Huang against the warm glow of the family room's lights. They appeared to be bent over a board game.

Ava hesitated at the bottom step and tugged nervously at the hem of her sweatshirt. "I'm not dressed for a party."

Alex raised her eyebrows. "And if I had given you more than five minutes before dragging you away, tell me what you would've worn. A pouffy dress? A flowy blouse?"

"You don't need to be so sassy." Ava crossed her arms and sighed. "I would've worn my Tigers jersey. And yes, I know to you it's not much different from this navy sweatshirt, but to me it is."

Alex grinned at her twin and straightened her short flowered skirt, crop top, and heather-gray cardigan. Alex loved getting dressed up, but she didn't care what Ava wore tonight. She was just happy that her sister was here. Ever since losing yesterday's game, Ava had spent much of her time curled up next to their Australian shepherd, Moxy, on the sofa, moping. She even refused to lick the bowl after Alex had baked brownies to bring tonight. That meant she was seriously bummed.

"You look fine. It's not really a party. Well, I guess it is, but the guys don't know that, so they won't be dressed up," Alex explained. Lindsey had been texting her all day, and in between doing her homework and buying a gift for Coach Jen, Alex had helped her plan the big surprise for Corey.

"Were we supposed to bring a present? I've never been to a two-month anniversary party," Ava admitted.

Alex snorted. "And you think I have?" She

held up the foil-covered brownie pan. "Here's our present."

"Works for me." Ava reached out to ring the doorbell. "I hope this party is worth it. I was into my cartoon marathon."

"It'll be great," Alex assured her, as Emily and Lindsey flung open the door.

"Come see! Come see!" Lindsey grabbed Alex's arm, dragging her down the narrow hall and into the kitchen.

"Tell your dad that was one great game," Mr. Campbell said in place of a greeting to Alex. "Is he going to go heavy on the defense down in Austin?"

"Thanks." She grinned, then admitted, "I have no idea." Why did people think her family sat around planning high school football strategy? Mr. Campbell was a lawyer. She doubted that he lectured Emily about courtroom strategy at the dinner table.

"Dad!" Emily raised her eyebrows meaningfully at him.

Mr. Campbell chuckled. "Okay, okay, I get it. The pizza chef does not talk to the guests. Are you ready for me to put this batch in the oven?"

"We made personal pizzas," Emily explained to Alex. "*Really* personal."

Alex peered at the small pizzas arranged on the baking pans. In addition to the usual mozzarella cheese and sauce, Emily and Lindsey had used thin slices of green peppers to spell out L + C 4EVER on every pie.

"That's so creative," Alex said. She silently wondered if having it on every pie wasn't a bit much. If Corey were her boyfriend, she'd only put it on the pizza she'd made for him. *But he's not my boyfriend*, she reminded herself. She'd never had a boyfriend. Who was she to judge?

"He'll really see how much you like him, Lindz," Alex said.

"I do, you know. Like him, that is." Lindsey's cheeks flushed pink.

"You guys are good together," Alex said. "And the house looks great. I saw the red balloons and streamers in the living room."

"Just like you said, since red is his favorite color," Lindsey agreed. "And look at the cake I made!"

Lindsey pulled the dome off a cake pan to reveal a heart-shaped cake frosted with red icing. Skittles spelled out L + C 4 EVER on the cake.

Alex had to hand it to Lindsey. She'd definitely gone all out, and her enthusiasm was really kind of sweet. She just hoped Ava wouldn't start giggling when she saw all this. Ava would never understand.

"They're all coming up the front walk!" Rosa yelled from the family room. "Hurry!"

Alex, Emily, and Lindsey raced into the family room. They peeked out the window. Corey, Logan, Xander, Andy Baker, and Jack Valdeavano pushed and shoved one another good-naturedly as they approached the house.

The girls gathered by the door.

"Ready?" Emily whispered to Lindsey.

Lindsey flung open the door before the doorbell rang. "Surprise!" she cried.

"Surprise!" Alex, Emily, Rosa, Annelise, and Charlotte echoed. Ava stood back, watching with an amused grin.

Lindsey leaped forward and snapped a red party hat on Corey's head.

"What's this?" Corey asked, startled.

"Is it your birthday, dude?" Andy demanded.

"No way," Corey said. "Hey, this isn't a loser party to make us feel better for the game yesterday, is it?"

"That would be classic." Jack punched Corey in the arm. Jack played soccer, and he always gave Corey and Ava a hard time about football. "Our team celebrates when we *win*."

"It's not a loser party!" Ava called out.

"Better not be," Andy muttered.

"Lindz?" Corey turned to her. "What's up?"

"It's our anniversary!" Lindsay sang out. "Two months together!"

Alex watched confusion reveal itself in Corey's blue eyes. He blinked rapidly, as if trying to process how this event related to the red party hat perched on his head.

"We're having a party," Alex explained, desperate to fill the silence. All the boys stared, dumbfounded. Lindsey beamed. Corey seemed a bit unsteady. "We're all going to celebrate our friends. Three cheers for Corey and Lindsey!"

Alex grabbed Lindsey's hand and Corey's and raised them together in the air, as she led the cheer. "Pretty good for a failed cheerleader, huh?" she teased.

"I'm not getting this," Logan said as they all moved into the family room.

"Is it like a wedding?" Xander asked.

"It is not like a wedding!" Corey said.

"Totally not," Lindsey agreed. "It's just a Corey-Lindsey party."

"I always wanted to go to one of those," cracked Jack.

"You should. You should always want to celebrate me!" Corey crowed, suddenly returned to his joking self.

The boys teased him, but Corey expertly deflected their jokes. Lindsey's face glowed as she snuggled beside Corey on the sofa. She rested her hand on his arm.

Alex sat cross-legged on the floor and talked to Charlotte, who was also new to Ashland. Alex felt awkward around the boys. She could speak at a school assembly, no problem, but one-on-one with a boy, her tongue seemed to adhere to the roof of her mouth. Debating the pros and cons of different shoes with Charlotte was a much safer option.

"Are you guys going to Austin?" Jack asked Ava.

"Definitely," Ava said.

"My family is going," Jack said. "My dad and uncle are football obsessed."

"Us too," said Andy. PJ Kelly was his cousin.

"We're all going too," Lindsey added. So did Emily and Rosa.

Alex couldn't believe how many kids who didn't have brothers on the team planned to make the trip to Austin.

"The whole town is going," Corey explained. "Everyone wants to see the big game. Ashland is taking over three hotels on the same street."

"Party in Austin!" Logan cried.

"You know it!" Corey cheered. Everyone talked excitedly about Austin. Corey planned a party in his hotel room.

Then Lindsey brought the pizzas out.

The boys fidgeted uncomfortably, staring in silent wonder at the message. No one had ever celebrated an anniversary. Most had never kissed a girl. Or even held hands. No one knew how to react.

"Ta-da!" Lindsey cried.

For a moment, Corey gripped the sofa pillow so tightly that Alex watched his knuckles go white. Then, just as quickly, he composed himself as he realized all eyes were on him, gauging his reaction. He threw the pillow at Jack's smirking face.

"Yum! Peppers!" he cried. He pulled up a pepper strip and sucked it into his mouth with a big slurp.

"Do you like the pizzas?" Lindsey asked. "Aren't they great?"

Rosa and Annelise agreed they were fantastic. Corey continued slurping peppers. Soon the other boys joined in. Even Ava slurped down a few as if they were gummy worms. They competed to see who could slurp fastest, and within minutes, all the peppers were gone.

Alex was impressed. Corey had skillfully erased the anniversary message without upsetting Lindsey. Lindsey sat beside him, eating pizza, as happy as ever, and everyone began to play a trivia game.

Alex excused herself and found the guest bathroom by the back stairs off the kitchen. When she emerged, she heard a whispered voice.

"Come on, Mom. Please?"

Alex froze in the doorway. The voice belonged to a boy.

"No, I feel fine. That's not it."

Alex realized that someone would only make a phone call back here if he wanted privacy. Should she let him know she could hear him?

"I can't stay here. Really, Mom, I can't. No, I know you aren't home. Yes. I know Logan's mom said she would drive home. But—"

Alex couldn't help herself. She peeked out the door. Corey sat hunched on the stairs, cradling his phone.

"Please, Mom, it's weird here."

Alex gulped and edged closer. Corey didn't sound like himself. He was usually in control and always joking.

"Yeah, fine. I'll keep to the plan. Bye."

Before Alex could react, Corey hurried down the stairs and collided with her. "Oh, hey, whoa!" He reached out for her shoulders to steady both of them.

"Hi," Alex said nervously, hyperaware of the warmth of his hands through her sweater.

"What are you doing back here?" he asked, pulling away.

"Bathroom." Alex pointed to the door. "I didn't mean to . . . I mean, it wasn't on purpose . . . I'm sorry, but I heard you on the phone. Are you okay?"

He shifted uneasily, assessing Alex. "Yeah, fine."

"Big surprise, huh?" Alex tried to lighten his mood.

"Huge." Corey shook his head. "It's nice and all. Lindsey's really nice, it's just weird, right?"

Alex bit her lip. "Weird how?"

"Weird that all the guys are supposed to be celebrating the anniversary of our going out for two months." He kept shaking his head. "Don't tell her, but I didn't even remember that."

"I won't tell," Alex promised. "I kind of knew the party was a bit much. Not your style."

He looked amused. "What's my style?"

Alex folded her arms. "Something simpler. More low-key. Chili dogs at Humphrey's?"

"Now that sounds good." He grinned at her and then looked away quickly. "It's hard to spell out anything on a chili dog."

"True." She thought about tipping him off about the Skittles on the heart-shaped cake, then decided not to. He'd surely bolt, and then Lindsey would be devastated.

They were quiet for a moment. Alex searched for something to say. It had been so easy talking to Corey for the past few minutes, but she was starting to feel awkward, like she usually did. She was grateful when he spoke again.

"Listen, please don't tell Lindsey about all this," Corey said, still not looking at her. "Don't tell her I got freaked out, okay?"

"Of course not." Alex liked how much he

cared about Lindsey's feelings. Corey really was a good guy. "We should probably go back."

"Onward!" Corey sauntered through the kitchen and back into the party. "Are we still doing trivia?" he called out. No one would ever have guessed that he wasn't having the best time.

Alex lingered in the kitchen. She arranged her brownies on a plate and stared at the cake.

"I was looking for you," Lindsey said, coming in a few minutes later. "Let's bring out dessert. I can't wait to see Corey's face when I present the cake!"

"About that." Alex nervously cleared her throat. "Maybe we should change the cake. Take off the words? You could even slice it in here?"

"Why would I want to do that?" Lindsey asked. She tucked a piece of her shiny hair behind her ear.

"Did you know that Corey doesn't like Skittles?" Alex asked. She had no idea if this was true. She was grasping here. She'd promised Corey not to tell Lindsey that she was freaking him out.

"Really?" Lindsey tilted her head, searching her memory. "Who doesn't like Skittles?"

"Corey. He hates them. Ava told me." Alex hated lying, but she could not let Lindsey walk out with that cake.

"But it's the message that counts," Lindsey protested. "It doesn't matter that I used Skittles."

"Oh, yes, it does," Alex insisted. "Your choice of candy will show him that you don't really know him."

"You think?" Lindsey screwed up her nose. After a moment of consideration, she called for Emily. She frantically explained the Skittles problem.

Emily searched her pantry. "We don't have any other little candies. Would Cheerios work? Or sunflower seeds?"

"Gross!" Lindsey cried.

"Look," Alex said, trying to sound reasonable. "Corey knows how much you like him. I think the heart-shaped cake gets the message across loud and clear. We can pick off the Skittles and smooth out the frosting. Besides, wouldn't you rather be out there with him than wasting time in the kitchen with us?"

"Oh, Alex!" Lindsey wrapped her in a hug. "You are the best friend, and you are so right."

Alex hugged Lindsey back. After all these

months, Lindsey was finally starting to treat her the way she treated Emily, who had been her best friend since first grade. Alex smiled as she began to pick off the Skittles. She'd done this for Lindsey even more than for Corey. She wanted this party to end well. She wanted her new best friend to be happy.

Where did Alex go? Ava wondered. She'd walked away during the trivia game and never returned. Emily and Lindsey had disappeared into the kitchen, and Rosa and Annelise had left for the bathroom. She and Charlotte remained in the family room with the boys. Ava didn't mind. She had more to say to them than she did to Rosa and Annelise.

"Do you think Coach Kenerson is angry?" Logan asked, reaching for a handful of chips.

"If he is, he's angry at all of us," Xander said. "We didn't play well."

"Some of us played worse than others," Andy said. He brushed his hand over his spiky, white-blond crew cut.

"What's that mean?" Corey demanded.

"I mean that some of us hold more blame." Andy crossed his beefy arms. "I did my part."

"Are you talking about me?" Corey challenged, leaning in toward Andy.

"No." Andy let his gaze land on Ava.

"Me? You're pinning the blame on me?" Ava widened her eyes.

"You didn't make the kick." Andy shrugged.

"That was an impossible kick," Corey retorted, coming to her defense.

"It was," Charlotte agreed, even though Ava was certain she knew nothing about football.

"One kick and we'd be going on to the championships," Andy sneered. "Just saying."

On the field and at home, Ava had felt responsible and sad. Now she was angry. Ever since the first practice, Andy had resented having her on the football team because she was a girl. He was the only one who couldn't move beyond that.

"One more *touchdown* and we'd be going to the championship," Ava shot back. "There was that missed opportunity in the second quarter, wasn't there?" She stared at Andy. He knew she was referring to the ball he'd failed to catch. She wasn't giving him the satisfaction of rattling her, especially in front of the other guys. Besides, who was Andy Baker to make the whole loss her fault?

"Whoa!" Corey waved his arms. "Everyone chill out. That game is over. Done. *Finito*. Next year will be our year to go all the way."

"You got it," Andy agreed. "And we won't have to worry about Ava kicking for us."

"What are you talking about?" Ava demanded. Andy made her so angry! Did he really think she wouldn't make the team next year? She could run and kick circles around him.

"I'm talking about the game in Austin," Andy said with a self-satisfied grin. "If your dad can't bring home the State Championship trophy, the town will fire him. Coach Sackett and your whole family will be out of Ashland for good."

"Are you crazy?" Xander cried, jumping to his feet. "The Tigers are not going to lose."

"Yeah, you can't even think that." Corey shook his head. "The high school guys have the game in the bag."

"The Tigers are going to win, for sure," Jack agreed. He turned to Ava. "You're not going anywhere."

"I know that," Ava scoffed. "Andy's talking crazy."

"Dessert time!" Lindsey's voice rang out. She carried out a heart-shaped cake. Alex and Emily trailed in with the plate of brownies. The boys dove into the sweets.

Ava sat back, turning over in her head what Andy had said. On Friday night she'd believed that the Tigers would easily win the big game. Her dad was a great coach, and the Tigers were a skilled team. But after her own game yesterday, she saw that sometimes the talent and training didn't come together. What if the Tigers lost in Austin? Would Coach be fired? Would they have to move to a different town?

Her stomach tightened. She'd miss everyone here. Maybe not Andy, but everyone else. She liked living in Ashland. She belonged here.

She needed to talk to Coach.

CHAPTER FOUR

"Attention, class!" Madame Knowlton rapped her knuckles on her desk on Monday at school.

Alex looked up from the poster she and Charlotte were coloring.

"She's not adding something else, is she?" Logan groaned next to her.

Madame Knowlton, their French teacher, was famous for assigning a project and then adding a new part to it each day. Alex found this infuriating. She liked knowing what was what before she started.

At least I have Charlotte, Jack, and Logan in my group, she thought.

Usually group projects were torturous, and

Alex ended up doing all the work. She knew she shouldn't, but rarely did anyone do things exactly the way she thought they should be done. Her mom had warned her over and over that she was too much of a perfectionist. Even now, she had to try super hard not to criticize the haphazard way Charlotte was coloring the cow's spots. Each group had to create their own restaurant, with a complete menu and poster in French. They'd named their restaurant La Petite Vache—or the Little Cow.

Madame Knowlton adjusted her round, wire-framed glasses on her long nose and fidgeted until the class quieted down. "Remember that we have a test tomorrow."

"I have two other quizzes tomorrow," Jack grumbled.

Alex nodded. She also had a ton of home-work and had forgotten about this test.

"The test will cover the vocabulary in this French restaurant unit, including all the new verbs, and you will need to know the conjuga-tions," Madame Knowlton explained. "Use this study guide." She passed out a stapled packet of paper just as the bell rang.

"Let's go to the media center now and do the

study guide together," Charlotte suggested to their group. French was their last-period class.

"I can't—wait, I can." Logan shook his head in amazement. "No more football practice this year. That's weird."

"I can stay until the late bus too," Jack said.

"Alex, what about you?" Charlotte asked.

Alex wasn't a fan of group study sessions. She studied better on her own. She didn't need their help. "I have to see Ms. Palmer about the student council bake sale."

"How long will that take?" Charlotte asked. "Couldn't you meet us after? Come on, it'll be fun."

"We need to finish writing our cow menu too." Jack held up the half-finished menu. They'd created a menu with all beef and dairy dishes.

"*Oui*," Alex agreed in French. She slung her backpack over her shoulder. "I'll see you there."

She hurried down the hall. First she stopped at the main office to hand in the money from the raffle she'd organized for the cheerleaders. Then she found Ms. Palmer, who was locking up her classroom.

"Hi, Alex, I'm glad you caught me. My son has a doctor's appointment, so I need to go." Ms. Palmer adjusted a folder of quizzes to grade in her canvas tote bag. Alex wondered if hers was one of them. She had Ms. Palmer for English.

"Okay, I just wanted to know what I should do to get ready for the bake sale. It's this Friday," Alex said.

"We have a student council meeting on Wednesday. It would be great if you made a sign-up sheet to pass out and organized the volunteers." Ms. Palmer smoothed her frizzy hair with her palms as they walked back down the hall together.

"About that meeting," Alex began. "I don't love a lot of the ideas for the Variety Show."

That was an understatement. Alex thought most of the ideas were horrendous, but she knew that she couldn't come right out and say that. The Variety Show was a yearly talent show organized around a central theme. Students and teachers performed skits, dances, songs, and even magic acts, and the goal was to draw in a big crowd from the town to raise a lot of money for student activities. Last week the student council had brainstormed ideas for a theme, and they would put them to a vote on Wednesday.

Alex thought about the lame ideas. Princesses. Magical Creatures. Ninjas. Oh, please!

"The student council is a democracy," Ms. Palmer explained while heading toward the main doors. "Each one of you was voted in by your grade, and each one of you has one vote. I can't get involved in campaigning for a theme."

"So if I think my theme is the best, I should campaign for it?" Alex asked. She hadn't considered this approach.

"Not formally. But you could talk to the other student council members and try to convince them to see the show your way." Ms. Palmer waved and hurried off toward her car.

I will make them see that my idea is the best, Alex decided as she walked into the media center. She spotted Charlotte, Jack, and Logan in the back corner by the reference books. A half-completed study guide and a copy of their French textbook lay on the round table in front of them. Jack chewed the eraser on his pencil as he debated with Logan the proper conjugation of *manger*, the verb for "to eat."

"It's *vous mangez*," Alex said as she pulled up a chair.

Charlotte flipped through the textbook. "Alex is right."

Alex bounced her knee impatiently. She was great at conjugating verbs. She didn't need to be here. She had so many other things to do.

She slid out her phone as they continued to fill in the conjugations on the study guide.

She texted Chloe Klein, the sixth-grade class president.

Think of all the great skits that go with Adventure of a Lifetime.

I still like Under the Sea.

Alex didn't want to knock Chloe's idea. Compared to the others, Under the Sea wasn't terrible.

Our ideas are so much better than the others.

For sure!

There are so many songs, skits,
and dances you can do about
adventure. Roller coasters, safaris,
road trips, etc. Nothing more
exciting than adventure!

Maybe. I'll think on it.

OK.

Alex planned to text her back tonight.

She texted Nate Nielson next. Then Tessa
Jones. She easily convinced Nate to toss Ninjas
as a theme and get on board with Adventure
of a Lifetime. Tessa refused to let go of Magical
Creatures, but finally she did waver. *A waver is
a start,* Alex thought. Alex decided to text Tessa
back tonight too. She still had five more student
council members to track down. Convincing
everyone was going to take a lot of time.

"Alex? Are you paying attention?" Charlotte
asked.

"Yes. No. Sorry." Alex raised her head.

They'd completed another chunk of the study guide without her. "Was that vocab you were reviewing?"

"Kind of, but there was a new part—" Charlotte reached for the paper.

"Wait a sec." Alex looked down at a text from Lindsey.

Corey acted weird today.

Weird how?

IDK. Just weird.
What should I do???

Why are you asking me?

You give good boy advice.

"Lindsey thinks I give good boy advice," she

whispered to Charlotte. She showed her the texts. She didn't want Logan and Jack to hear, but she was kind of proud.

"What are you going to tell her to do?" Charlotte whispered back.

Alex had no idea. She wasn't even sure what Lindsey was talking about. All of a sudden her ringtone started blaring, causing Ms. Majumder to abruptly stop shelving books. The librarian gave Alex the *no phones in the library* glare.

"Be right back," Alex told Charlotte as she scurried into the hall. "Hello?" she answered the call.

"Hello, this is Mercury Grill calling Alexandra Sackett about making a reservation," said a woman with a sugary accent on the other end.

"Right!" Alex lowered her voice to sound more grown-up. She booked the date and the time for dinner in Austin after the game. Her mom was going to be so happy and so surprised.

"We need a credit card number to hold the reservation, darlin'," the woman said sweetly.

"A credit card?" Alex didn't have a credit card. She promised the woman to get her a number later.

"We'll need you to call back within forty-eight

hours with a credit card number or we will release the reservation. Okay, darlin'?" the woman said.

"Sure, no problem." Alex would ask her dad for his number tonight. She ended the call, and her phone immediately buzzed again. It was Lindsey.

U still there????

Yep. Can we talk 2nite?
Crazy right now.

K. Don't forget!!

"Hey, Alex!"

Alex turned to see a man in a dark blazer and yellow tie standing before her. "Yes?" She didn't think she knew him.

"I'm Mr. Hess, the middle school athletic director. I was told by Mrs. Gusman in the office that you're the student I need to see." He pointed his finger at her.

"Me?"

"The middle school Booster Club wants to support the high school team at the State Championships. By the way, I'm a huge fan of your dad's pass-rush bluff." He paused, but when she didn't respond, he continued. "We want a big banner to fly at the game. We want to show our support."

"Great idea. One of those shiny, silky banners?" she asked.

"See? I knew Mrs. Gusman would get me to the right student." He handed Alex a piece of paper. "These are the instructions from the printer. Do you think you could design the banner for us and submit it online to the printer? Mrs. Gusman said you have access to the student council's account with that printer."

"Sure, I can." Alex found herself agreeing before she stopped to think. Besides the student council Variety Show campaign she had to wage, the boy advice for Lindsey she'd have to fake, and the piles of homework and studying she had to tackle, she was agreeing to make a banner. The more she did, the more people seemed to ask her to do.

"You're the best, Alex Sackett." Mr. Hess

grinned at her before striding down the hall.

"Thanks!" she called, then turned to see Charlotte, Jack, and Logan heading out of the media center. "Where are you guys going?"

"The late bus is coming," Jack said. "Besides, we finished the study guide."

"Sorry I didn't help." Alex felt bad.

"You were busy." Charlotte shrugged. "And we know you'll do well anyway."

"I better get my backpack before Ms. Majumder locks the media center doors." Alex reached for the door's handle.

Charlotte held up her packet. "Do you want to copy down our answers, just in case?"

Alex shook her head. "No, I'm okay. I never use study guides. I'll review on my own. I've got it all under control."

Ava glanced at the kids waiting for the late bus in the front hallway. She dropped her gym bag filled with gear and shifted her bulging laundry bag away from her body. It did not smell pleasant—probably because she'd waited until the end of the season to bring home the last month's worth of dirty football clothes from her gym locker.

She groaned. Sometimes she wished she wasn't such a slob. Alex would've cleaned out her locker every day. Alex probably would've ironed her uniform, then sprayed it with honeysuckle body mist!

"Hey, Sackett!" Corey headed toward her, followed by Xander and Bryce. They carried gym bags, but nothing like her overstuffed laundry bag. *Whatever,* she thought. *My bag can't smell any worse than they normally do. They won't notice.*

"Hey, yourself," she called back. She dropped the bag to the floor and slid down beside it. The boys sprawled next to her.

"Ugh! I smell salt-and-vinegar potato chips covered in spoiled milk," Corey said.

I guess I was wrong, Ava thought.

"You must be remembering lunch," Bryce joked. "That cafeteria odor is nasty."

"Especially on taco day," Ava added.

"Whoa, Sackett, it's you who reeks," Xander said, holding his nose.

"I'm trying out a new perfume. Scent of fermented football. Like it?" She reached out her arm.

"Get back. I'm going to hurl!" Xander pretended to vomit.

Ava rolled her eyes. "New topic. So are we doing that team pizza thing?"

"Not happening," Bryce said. "The football banquet is Thursday night. That'll be our big party."

"Corey here already had his party." Xander shot a braces rubber band at Corey.

"Hey, yeah, I heard about that. Heart cake, man!" Bryce guffawed.

"Lindsey is crazy into you." Xander shook his head in amazement. Then he shot a second rubber band.

"Crazy is right. She's totally intense," Corey said.

"Intense?" Ava asked. As soon as the question left her mouth, she wished she could take it back. She didn't want to hear about Lindsey and Corey's relationship.

"She texts me nonstop. She texts me to say good morning before I even roll out of bed. She texts me when she brushes her teeth. She texts me when she leaves the house for the bus. She texts me to say she's at the bus stop. Then when she's on the bus. It never stops. All day long!" Corey said.

"I guess she likes to text." Ava shrugged.

"And she's always sending me photos of food," Corey said.

"Food?" asked Bryce. "What's that mean?"

"Beats me. She snaps photos of everything before she eats it. And she wants me to comment, but what's there to say about a turkey sandwich?" Corey complained.

"Maybe she's hungry?" Bryce ventured.

"That's another thing," continued Corey. "At lunch, she never orders french fries. She says they're unhealthy. But do you see who eats my french fries? It's definitely not me! Lindsey takes fry after fry."

"You're supposed to share fries with your girlfriend, dude," said Xander. "Don't you know anything?"

"I think she goes out with me just to nab my fries," Corey said, a glint in his eye.

"Well, that makes sense." Ava smirked. "I can't imagine what else she sees in you. It's not your looks or your personality. Greasy potatoes, now that I understand."

"Real funny, Sackett." Corey grabbed one of Xander's rubber bands off the ground and flung it at her.

"Girls get crazy about everything," Bryce complained. "My sisters go nuts if you don't go all out on their birthdays. It's like they think they're royalty or celebrities or something."

"Oh, wow. When is Lindsey's birthday?" Corey looked panicked.

"Burn, man. You are in trouble!" Xander pumped his fist.

"Look what she did for you for two months of going out. She's going to expect her birthday to be epic," Ava agreed.

Corey hung his head. "Why do girls have to be like that, Sackett?"

"Yeah, why can't they be chill like us?" Bryce waved his arm to indicate the four of them sprawled on their smelly laundry.

And Ava couldn't hold back her grin. She was no longer the lone girl on the football team. She was now one of the guys.

CHAPTER FIVE

"Say 'Austin!'" Alex called during lunch on Wednesday. She framed the photo of Lindsey and Corey and clicked. "Let's do a couple more. Corey, move in closer."

The shine of lip gloss highlighted Lindsey's white teeth as she flashed an effortless smile. Her blond hair fell in soft waves to her shoulders. It was hard not to focus on her—she was so confidently pretty.

Yet as she lined up the pictures on Lindsey's phone, Alex found her own gaze stuck on Corey's eyes. It wasn't the bright blue color that reminded her of the ocean, but the flicker of uncertainty she saw there. His mouth was smiling, but his eyes weren't. Was he as self-conscious as she was in front of the camera? She always felt stiff, as if she were trying too hard.

Alex shook her head. Why was she grouping herself with Corey? Corey and Lindsey were perfect. The perfect football player. The perfect cheerleader. The perfect couple.

Rosa leaned on the cafeteria table and peered over Alex's shoulder at the camera. "What's with the cutesy photo shoot?"

"Yeah." Corey stopped smiling. "Why are we doing this again?"

Lindsey's gaze flicked to Alex. Alex was ready for this question. "It's for the yearbook," Alex said.

"Cool!" Corey stuck out his tongue. "Take this one."

"What about me?" Logan protested. "Don't I get to be in the yearbook?"

"Who are you going out with?" Emily asked.

"No one. What's that got to do with anything?" Logan demanded.

"The yearbook is doing a cutest couples page," Alex explained, feeling a lump lodged in her throat as she spoke. She wasn't even on the yearbook. Of course, no one questioned this part of the story that Lindsey had fabricated. Alex was involved in everything else in the school, so why not the yearbook?

Alex paused for a moment to consider this. Maybe she should join the yearbook.

"We're a couple," Xander announced, wrapping his arm around Charlotte.

"In your dreams!' Charlotte wriggled away from Xander. "I'm not taking a photo with you."

"Xander, you're not cute enough to be on the page," Lindsey teased, smiling at Corey.

"Yeah, check out my face. Model material!" Corey bragged. Alex quickly snapped another photo.

Guilt enlarged the lump in her throat. She swallowed painfully. These photos were never going in the yearbook. Lindsey had cooked up this fake photo shoot so she could make Corey a surprise online scrapbook. Alex couldn't understand Lindsey's desire to broadcast her relationship. What did she have to prove? Everyone knew she and Corey were meant for each other. No one needed to see it displayed on a pizza or an online scrapbook.

At first Lindsey had planned to do one large photo. Instead Alex had suggested shooting a bunch of silly photos—kind of like the strip of photos from a photo booth. As they talked, the idea morphed to a romantic online scrapbook. Alex had spent hours on the phone with Lindsey and Emily, planning the photos.

"Let's take one more," Lindsey suggested.

"All of us this time!" Rosa cried. She, Xander, and Logan gathered alongside Lindsey.

"No! No!" Lindsey's voice came out shrill. "Just me and Corey."

"The yearbook is not just about you and Corey," Rosa pointed out.

Lindsey ignored Rosa and wrapped her arm possessively around Corey's shoulder. "How about nose to nose?"

"How about not?" Corey pulled back, as Lindsey pressed her nose against his. "Why can't everyone be in it? Alex, isn't this your thing?"

"Uh, uh . . . ," Alex stammered. It wasn't *her* thing. She wanted to help Lindsey, but she hated lying. Plus, she had an English vocabulary quiz next period that she'd planned to study for during lunch. She handed Lindsey back her phone. "Actually, I'm all set!"

"Me too." Corey stalked toward the trash can with his balled-up paper bag. An awkward silence fell over their lunch table.

Alex pulled out her sheet of vocabulary words. The letters ran together as she frantically tried to memorize. Why hadn't she studied last night? She'd spent too much time on the phone with Lindsey and texting the student council members. She wondered how the Variety Show vote would go today. She had Nate and Carly Hermano on her side. Chloe, maybe.

"So what do you think? It went well, right? I mean, Corey seemed a little angry at the end, but that was because Rosa was being pushy." Lindsey sat beside Alex. "He's going to be so into me when he sees the scrapbook."

"Lindsay, he's *already* into you. I really need to review these words." Alex held up the sheet.

"You're so smart. You always do great on vocabulary." Lindsey gave her a sincere smile that calmed Alex's panic. "You'll ace it."

She's right, Alex told herself as the bell rang. She followed the tide of kids down the hall to English class. *I have this!*

But when she handed in her quiz to Ms. Palmer at the end of class, Alex was sure of one thing: She didn't have this. At all. She'd never been so lost on a vocabulary quiz in her life. Why had it been so hard?

Her stomach clenched. She feared how bad her grade would be. She sat through math class in a daze. What would Ms. Palmer think? Alex had always excelled in her class.

"You okay?"

Alex started, surprised to find Corey by her side as she walked mechanically out of math toward French.

"You look upset." His usually pompous, jokey personality was replaced with concern.

"I'm fine." For a moment, Alex thought about telling him about the quiz, but her failure was too embarrassing to share. She didn't want his pity. She kept her head down and hurried into French class.

"*Bonjour!*" Madame Knowlton's cheery voice rang out.

Alex shook herself free of her foul mood. She turned her attention to the translation flashed onto the smart board. She liked French class. Everything was going to be fine. It always was.

Two minutes before the final bell ended the school day, Madame Knowlton walked down the aisles, placing the graded tests that they'd taken yesterday facedown on the desks.

Alex flipped hers over.

A red C scrawled in marker at the top of her test blurred and swam as tears pricked her eyes. She blinked them back, trying to process what she saw. She'd thought the B she'd gotten last week was bad. A C was unthinkable.

This had to be a mistake, she decided. She checked the paper, half expecting to see another student's name written on it. All she saw was *Alex Sackett* in her own rounded print.

"Alex, check me out. I got an A!" Charlotte leaned forward from the desk behind her. "Oh, wow." Charlotte had caught sight of Alex's paper. "I can't believe I got a better grade than you. That never happens. Now I'm doubly proud of myself."

"That's great," Alex said tightly. But it wasn't great. Alex always got the highest grades in the class. Something had to be wrong. Madame Knowlton had messed up.

She waited until everyone had left the classroom. She straightened her pale-blue plaid shirt and walked confidently up to Madame Knowlton's desk.

"*Bonjour*, Alex." Madame Knowlton smiled warmly. Teachers always loved her. She knew Madame Knowlton would apologize when she saw what she'd done to Alex.

"Can you please check to see if you made a mistake grading my test?" Alex smiled back and handed the teacher her test.

"I can check." Madame Knowlton raised her thin eyebrows. She adjusted her glasses, then scanned the test questions. "No, Alex. This is the grade you deserve."

"I don't deserve a C!" Alex's voice cracked. "I knew the vocabulary words. I knew the conjugations."

"But you didn't know the translation or the history of French cooking." Madame Knowlton pointed to a bunch of questions marked with nasty red x's.

"History of French cooking?" Alex had been confused when she'd seen that on the test. When had they done that in class? "We never reviewed that. No one could've known those answers."

"That information was on the study guide," her teacher reported.

"The study guide? You never said that!"

"I clearly told the class to complete the study guide," Madame Knowlton said.

"But I thought I didn't need to. I was busy that night. Besides, study guides are for kids who don't know everything," Alex protested.

"But you didn't know everything." Madame Knowlton folded her hands, as if the conversation were finished.

This was so unfair! Alex tried desperately to convince her teacher not to count those questions. Madame Knowlton wouldn't agree. Alex suggested a makeup test. Madame Knowlton refused. Alex begged for an extra-credit project. Again, Madame Knowlton turned her down.

"This is your grade," Madame Knowlton said. "Think of this experience as a learning tool. You now know that you need to use the study guides."

Alex didn't want a learning tool. She wanted her A. "B-but . . . but . . . ," she sputtered.

"It's one test, Alex." Madame Knowlton's voice grew warmer. "Have one of your parents sign it, and I'm confident you'll do better next time."

"Sign it?" Alex asked.

"Any student receiving a grade of C or below needs a parent's signature," the teacher explained. "That's the school policy, remember?"

I don't remember, because I never get Cs! Alex wanted to shout. But she didn't. How mortifying that she'd have to show this grade to her mom and dad. She wanted to crumple the test and shove it in the trash.

"What if I correct all my mistakes, and you give me half credit for each one?" Alex offered.

Madame Knowlton held up her hands. "No deal."

"One-third credit?" Alex tried.

"No more negotiating, Alex." The teacher pointed her toward the door.

Alex sighed. Could this week get any worse?

She wandered down the quiet hallway toward the front of the school. She texted her mom that she'd take the late bus home. Then she stopped in the media center and used the computer to submit the design for the Booster Club banner, all the while seething over Madame Knowlton's study guide trick and the fact that she had to have a parent sign her test. She wouldn't dare bother her dad. He was stressed over the championship game, and it was still over a week away. She hoped her mom would see the injustice.

"What were you doing in *there*?"

Alex had stepped out of the media center and nearly collided with Chloe.

"I was just"—Alex blinked, suddenly realizing that it was Wednesday afternoon—"Oh no! Did I miss the student council meeting?"

"Yes! You finally convinced me last night me to vote for your Variety Show theme. I gave up my perfectly good idea to vote for yours, and then you don't even show up!" Chloe narrowed her dark eyes. "I don't get you."

"I needed to talk with a teacher." Alex pressed her hand against her forehead. How had she forgotten this meeting, of all meetings? "Did Adventure of a Lifetime win?"

"Seriously? Without you there to talk it up? Everyone figured you didn't care or were angry or something." Chloe adjusted her book bag. "We're doing Sage's idea. Wild Wild West. At least it's better than Tessa's Magical Creatures. It was close, Alex."

Alex groaned. Her idea had been so good.

"And Ms. Palmer was looking for you, because you were supposed to coordinate the bake sale," Chloe added. "She seemed kind of annoyed."

Alex cringed. The sign-up sheet she'd made last night was tucked in her backpack. "I'm sorry. Is Ms. Palmer still here?"

Chloe pointed out the huge glass windows by the main office. "There's no time, Alex. The late buses are about to leave." Chloe sprinted out the door. The buses revved their engines.

Alex had no choice. She had to get on her bus. She'd apologize to Ms. Palmer tomorrow. What a mess!

"Well, look who's here!" Mrs. Sackett put down her fork and grinned at her husband.

"Coach!" Ava cried with delight. She'd barely seen him since the weekend, and it was now Wednesday night. He'd been at the school and on the field preparing for the big game.

"I was craving a home-cooked meal," he said, closing the back door. He dropped his bag, washed his hands, and pulled out his chair at the table. Then he reached over and ruffled Alex's and Ava's hair.

"Daddy! Quit it!" Alex brushed his hand away.

Coach had been doing this since they were babies. Even though she was probably too old for it, Ava still liked it. She didn't care if he messed up her hair. But Alex hated having her hair touched. Plus, Alex had been grumpy all day.

Coach lifted the serving bowl of pasta. "Got here just in time, I see. The Eating Machine hasn't devoured everything."

"Yet," Ava said knowingly. Tommy's appetite was enormous. "He's building strength for Austin. Do you think you'll put him in?"

"Maybe," Coach said. "But he needs to improve his footwork. He's got to tighten the progression and solidify his base."

"True. Then he'll be more stable when he throws. How about some drills in the backyard?" Ava suggested.

"Hello? Do you two not see me sitting here?" Tommy waved his arms. "I'm sick of everyone talking about me like I'm some windup toy."

"No one is doing that, Tom." Coach took a big swig of iced tea and grinned at Ava. Ava knew he loved talking strategy with her.

Tommy sighed. "Yes, they are. In the halls of the high school. At the gas station. Today the school bus driver, some old guy in a fishing cap, shared his pass accuracy tips with me in front of the entire bus!" He pushed away his plate, which remained half-full. If Tommy wasn't eating, that meant he was sick or nervous. Ava was pretty sure it was the latter.

"Welcome to my world, Tom. Everyone in Ashland has an opinion or a strategy to share," Coach reported.

"Still?" Mrs. Sackett asked. "What could they possibly have to complain about now that we're going to State?"

"Everything." Coach shook his head. "For some people, winning isn't enough, if it's not done their way."

"Andy Baker said something to me the other day." Ava poked at a piece of pasta with her fork. She'd been waiting to get Coach alone, but she knew he'd retreat to his study after dinner to watch tapes of their opponents' games, trying to find their weak spots.

"PJ's cousin?" Mrs. Sackett asked.

"What did Andy say?" Alex spoke for the first time.

Ava wondered why Alex was so quiet. Tommy not eating meant he was worried. Alex not talking usually meant the same thing. But Alex couldn't be worried about the football game too. Could she?

"Oh, well, it's kind of silly. Andy was probably just saying it to be mean," Ava began.

"That's typical of him," Alex said.

"A family trait," Tommy agreed. He didn't like PJ much.

"Andy said that if the Tigers don't win in

Austin, Coach might be fired." Ava watched her dad, waiting for him to laugh at the silliness of Andy's statement.

But Coach met her mom's knowing gaze and held it across the table. And in that moment, Ava knew they'd discussed this topic before. And it wasn't silly.

"It won't come to that." Mrs. Sackett waved her hand dismissively.

"But could it?" Ava pressed.

"I won't lie to you." Coach's voice was controlled. "It's a possibility."

"But you brought the team to State!" Tommy cried. "What more do they want?"

"They want the big gold trophy. If I don't deliver that, they may or may not decide to keep me," Coach explained. "I only have a one-year contract with the school board. They wouldn't give me a longer one until I'd proven myself."

"It will all work out." Mrs. Sackett smiled brightly. "We'll hope for the best and think happy thoughts."

"Exactly. Is there more salad?" Coach asked, changing the subject.

But Ava couldn't think happy thoughts. As soon as dinner finished, she pulled Alex and

Tommy into the family room. Alex picked at her chipped pink nail polish. Ava had never seen her twin do this. Alex constantly polished her nails so they looked perfect.

"What's wrong?" Ava asked. "You don't seem to care that we're going to be kicked out of town."

"I have bigger problems," Alex mumbled.

"What's bigger than that?" Ava asked.

"My grades are horrible," Alex admitted, still staring at her nails.

"You? Miss Perfect?" Tommy chuckled.

"Stop it." Ava nudged her brother. "Al's exaggerating."

"No, I'm not. I got a C on a test today," Alex said.

"Hey, maybe we're more alike than people think," Ava teased, but then she saw Alex's grim look. "Sorry. I'm not making fun of you. I bet you're just having a bad week."

"Maybe." Alex shrugged.

"Let's talk about the game," Ava said urgently. "What if the team loses? What then?"

"I have no idea," Tommy said. "I'd hate to move again."

"Well, forget it. I am *not* moving. I like my friends. I like my team," Ava declared. "I fit in here."

"Me too," Alex agreed. "But it's not like we can do anything."

"What are you talking about?" Ava cried. "You're the queen of doing things. When the tornado tore up the football field, you rallied the whole town to fix it! And when Coach Byron didn't have anyone to watch his kids, you set up a babysitting ring!"

"That was a different time." Alex sighed dramatically. She seemed more interested in peeling the polish from her pinkie nail.

"Al, why aren't you into this? We need to get motivated. I can't just sit around and hope for the best." Ava turned to Tommy. "If they call you into the game, you need to score a lot of touchdowns."

"What if I can't do that?" Tommy asked. "Or what if I'm not called in? You can't pin this all on me."

Ava bit her lip. "Then we have to think of something else, because I refuse to leave. Operation Stay-in-Ashland begins now."

CHAPTER SIX

One more week. One more week. The phrase repeated in Ava's head all day on Thursday.

In one week, she and Alex would leave Ashland to drive to Austin with their mom. Coach and Tommy would travel on the high school bus. All schools in Ashland would close on Friday for the game. Back in Massachusetts, only a blizzard or an ice storm closed the schools. But in Ashland many businesses planned to close too. The whole town was traveling to the game.

Only one week to come up with plan B, she thought. Plan A was winning the game. That was up to Coach and Tommy.

She couldn't think of *anything*.

And all anyone could talk about tonight was the big game. Of course, she was at the middle school football banquet, so that made sense.

"Are you going to eat that?" Corey asked.

Ava glanced down at the breaded chicken cutlet nestled next to limp green beans on her plate. "No. All yours." She pushed her plate over to him. Then she glanced across McBride's Family Restaurant. She watched her mom and Coach at one of the parents' tables. Coach scratched his head and smiled at something Mr. Browning said. Ava spotted the tightness in Coach's jaw. He could pretend to everyone that he was confident about the big game, but Ava knew better. She'd give him an extra-big hug before bed. He'd taken hours away from game preparation to sit with the know-it-all parents tonight. But he'd been there when Coach Kenerson presented her with the Hardest Worker Award.

"One hundred and ten percent!" her dad had called out, as he and her mom stood to applaud her. Coach had taught her to never give up.

Ava examined the plaque engraved with her name. She wouldn't give up on Ashland. She and this plaque were staying here. But how?

"What a blowhard!" Corey whispered to her.

"Huh? Who?" Ava whispered back.

Corey tilted his head toward Mr. Whittaker, who was standing by the dessert display. He gestured wildly with his hands as he spoke. Other men listened with rapt attention. "Mr. Whittaker. Just because he's superrich, he thinks he runs the show."

"What's he doing *here*?" Ava asked. "I thought he was president of the *high school* boosters."

"Mr. Whittaker says he's in charge of building future teams. If the preschool football kids had a juice and cookies party, Mr. Whittaker would be there," Corey said. "He makes all the football decisions in this town."

"Really?" Ava watched Mr. Whittaker. He wore a nice navy suit and shiny black cowboy boots. His silver hair fell in a swoop over his broad forehead. He stood with confidence.

"The man has mega-money, so everyone listens to him," Corey said.

Ava felt her brain begin to churn. "Did he hire my dad?"

"He probably okayed it." Corey shrugged. "I doubt they could've hired him if Floyd Whittaker said no."

Maybe they can't fire him either if Mr. Whittaker says no, she thought.

Ava knew then what she had to do. She waited until players began filing toward the dessert table laden with Texas sheet cake and cookies. As Mr. Whittaker stepped back to avoid the crowd, Ava planted herself right by his side.

"Hi, Mr. Whittaker." Ava extended her hand the way Coach had taught her.

Mr. Whittaker raised his silver eyebrows in surprise. "Hello, Little Sackett!" He pumped her arm up and down in a hearty shake. "Tough kick at the end of that last game. Not to worry. You'll grow. You'll get stronger. You'll kick longer. In a few years, that kick will be baby stuff."

Here was the opening she needed. Ava took a deep breath. "That's the thing, Mr. Whittaker. I really, really want to play for the Tigers."

"Of course you do. Every kid wants to be on our team." He let out a hearty laugh. "Living the dream!"

"I mean that it's super important that I stay in Ashland and go to high school in Ashland," Ava said.

"Great town. I was born here. I've lived my whole life here except for a stint over at Baylor in Waco. Doesn't get any better than Ashland." Mr. Whittaker beamed with pride. Then his gaze landed on Mayor Johnston, who was headed in their direction.

Ava tapped her foot nervously. He wasn't understanding her hints, and she didn't have much time. "What happens if the Tigers lose the State Championship?" she blurted. "What happens to us? My family?"

"Whoa!" Mr. Whittaker crossed his arms in front of him, as if warding off an evil spirit. "Don't you go jinxing things now. We are not going to lose, darlin'. Not at all." He turned and slapped the mayor on his back by way of a greeting. "Baxter! Talk to me about the new irrigation system for the lower fields. We've got to look to the future!"

Ava listened to the two men talk about sprinklers and water runoff issues. *What about my future? My family's future?* she wanted to cry. What good was Mr. Whittaker and all his money and power if she couldn't get him to promise he'd let them stay no matter what?

She needed to figure out another way.

Alex walked slowly through the empty hallways on Friday afternoon. She was missing a new lesson in French, but she couldn't bring herself to care. With that last test grade, she had no chance of pulling out an A for this marking period.

She folded the yellow pass as she walked to the main office, stopping to fashion it into an origami crane. Why had she been called to the office? Something with student council? She searched her brain but couldn't remember.

Alex yawned and tucked a stray piece of hair into her messy ponytail. She'd stayed up late studying for math and baking cookies for the bake sale. Then she'd arrived at school early to set up the bake sale table and display the treats. If she'd been at the meeting on Wednesday, she would've convinced more people to help. But getting volunteers via text was much harder.

"Good afternoon, Alex!" Mrs. Gusman, the school secretary, greeted her when Alex entered the bustling office. She narrowed her eyes. "Are you feeling okay?"

"Sure. Why?"

"Oh, nothing. It's just that you always wear such cute outfits. I love how you match your headband to your sweater or skirt. I'm just surprised to see you looking so . . ." Mrs. Gusman's voice trailed off.

Alex glanced down at her gray sweatpants and grungy pink sweatshirt. She didn't think she'd ever worn sweatpants to school. Sweats were for lazy kids, she liked to tell Ava. But this morning she couldn't find the energy to care about fashion. She would've come in her pajamas if she hadn't been wearing her fleece pants with dancing penguins.

Alex perched on the edge of Mrs. Gusman's desk, eager to change the subject. "How are O'Malley and Malarkey?"

Mrs. Gusman brightened and stopped typing. "At one in the morning last night, little Malarkey began to bark and bark. Scared me silly! I thought an intruder had broken in. Turns out that O'Malley snuck into Malarkey's bed. Two pugs in one little bed! It took an hour to sort out the sleeping situation."

"What silly dogs!" Alex said. Mrs. Gusman always told her O'Malley and Malarkey stories. She held up her paper crane pass. "Madame Knowlton said you wanted to see me."

Mrs. Gusman's smile faded. "We have a problem."

"We do?" Alex asked hesitantly.

Mrs. Gusman pulled open the top of a large

cardboard box. She unfurled an enormous banner made from shiny royal-blue-and-orange material. "The middle school Booster Club banner arrived."

"Great!" Alex stood to examine it. "Oh! Not great!" She gasped when she read the words embroidered on the banner: GO ASHLAND TIGGERS!

"Tiggers? Tiggers?" Alex found herself repeating the mistake.

"Same as the character in *Winnie the Pooh*. Do you know Tigger? My grandson used to bounce around like Tigger does." Mrs. Gusman smiled at the memory.

"But we're the Tigers!" Alex cried. "How could the printer make such a huge mistake?"

"Calm down, Alex." Mrs. Gusman rested her hand gently on Alex's arm. "We will solve this."

She picked up the phone and dialed a number. While she waited for an answer, she handed a parent a pass to retrieve her sick child from the nurse's office.

"Hello, this is Beatrice Gusman at the Ashland Middle School office, calling about the banner delivered today," she began. Then she told the printing company about the hideous mess-up. "Uh-huh. I see." Mrs. Gusman typed something, then squinted at her computer screen. "Yes, yes.

I agree. No, it will have to be fixed. We'll have to figure that part out. Thank you."

Mrs. Gusman hung up the phone and swiveled the screen so Alex could see.

Alex's stomach gave a sharp squeeze. The order form—the one she had filled out in the library and submitted—said *Tiggers*, not Tigers. She had made the typo. She had turned her dad's football team from fierce, fighting Tigers to silly, bouncing Tiggers! What if Mrs. Gusman hadn't opened the box before sending it on to Austin? She cringed at the thought.

"I never would have expected *you* to mess up, Alex," Mrs. Gusman mused.

"I'm so sorry." Alex felt terrible. "Truly I am. Will they fix it?"

"They will. They'll need to charge the Booster Club more money, though," Mrs. Gusman said quietly.

"But it's my fault." Alex's stomach squeezed so tightly, she held her side. "I should pay." Her piggy bank held about thirty dollars from her birthday. She wondered if her parents would let her take money out of her savings account.

"Let me try to work out the money with the printer on Monday." Mrs. Gusman turned to another parent signing out her son. "Mistakes happen to the best of us, Alex."

Except they've been happening to me a lot, Alex thought.

CHAPTER SEVEN

"You're still in your pajamas?" Mrs. Sackett's voice registered her surprise. "Do you feel okay?"

"I feel fine," Alex said. She clicked randomly through design websites on her computer. "It's still Saturday morning."

"Technically, for five more minutes." Mrs. Sackett motioned to the clock hands nearing noon. "You're usually up and at the library long before now."

Alex shrugged. "Not today."

Her mom stepped into her room. She surveyed the clothes draped on Alex's chair and dropped on her floor. She raised her eyebrows at the pages ripped from magazines littering her daughter's unmade bed. "Something's up. Messy and lazy do not describe the Alex I know."

"Maybe they do." Alex clicked on directions to decoupage a keepsake box. Earlier she'd spent two hours helping Lindsey design her online scrapbook for Corey. Alex still thought the whole thing was a bit much, but Lindsey wouldn't budge. She said it was important that Corey see how happy they were. She'd promised to forward Alex a copy when she sent it via Buddybook to Corey. *What will I do with a copy?* Alex wondered. Hey! She could decoupage a box with photo after photo of the smiling, happy couple.

Just what she needed.

Her mom smoothed the edge of Alex's comforter and sat. Normally Alex would cringe if her mom touched her bed with her black sweatpants, which crackled with dried clay—Mrs. Sackett had started a ceramics business in their garage—but today she barely registered it.

"You're awfully quiet. Let's talk," her mom prodded.

There's nothing to talk about, Alex thought. How could her mom possibly fix all the things she'd messed up? *Maybe my time for greatness has come and gone,* Alex realized suddenly. She'd read an article online a few weeks ago about girls who were super popular in high school and then went downhill from there. The article warned girls not to peak too early. *Maybe I've peaked at age twelve,* Alex thought. Maybe her schoolwork and her leadership skills were now on a downward spiral. She groaned.

Then she remembered the French test waiting for a signature in her backpack. Coach and Tommy were at a practice at the high school, and Ava was at the park with Jack. She braced herself as she handed the test to her mom without an explanation. She kept her head down so she wouldn't have to see the disappointment on her mom's face.

"I'm surprised," Mrs. Sackett said, watching Alex closely.

"You need to sign it. Okay?" Alex asked.

"Okay." Her mom reached for a pen and scrawled her name.

"Okay? That's it? No lecture or yelling?" Alex asked, looking up to see that her mom's face remained calm. Alex's cell phone buzzed, but she ignored it.

"Did you want a lecture?" Her mom smiled.

"You've always worked hard, and your grades have been spectacular. One C is fine, sunshine. Do you need me to help you with French?"

"No." Alex shoved the test into her backpack. Maybe the C was fine to her mom, but not to her.

"Is this why you're moping?" Mrs. Sackett asked.

"I'm not moping," Alex said. But she knew she was.

"Things will settle down around here after the football game next week. We all need some time to regroup." She smoothed Alex's hair from her face. "And you and I will have fun in Austin, I promise. Shopping and eating and—"

"Oh!" Alex cried, suddenly remembering the restaurant. "Can I have your credit card number?"

"I didn't mean shopping *right now*," Mrs. Sackett said.

"It's a surprise for you and Daddy. I'm not charging anything on it. It's just to hold something. I promise," Alex said.

Her mom agreed. Alex took her cell phone into the bathroom. She glanced at the screen. Five texts and a call from Lindsey. Lindsey would have to wait, she decided, and she called

Mercury Grill. She explained who she was and that she was confirming her reservation with a credit card.

The woman on the phone had a higher voice than the one she'd spoken with at the beginning of the week. "I'm sorry. Your reservation is no longer in the system, because you never called us with the credit card."

"But I have it now," Alex protested. "Can I make another reservation?"

"I'm sorry," the woman repeated. "We're fully booked for that night. Austin is packed. There's a big high school football game, did you know that?"

Alex couldn't believe she'd forgotten to call back. Her mom had been so nice about the bad grade, and Alex couldn't even get her into this restaurant. Alex hadn't thought she could feel any worse, but she'd been wrong.

"Three points!" Ava called.

"We're not playing points." Jack snatched the rebound, then sent the basketball toward the hoop. The orange ball bounced off the rim.

"We could. One-on-one and keep score," Ava offered. She zipped her hoodie as the first cool breeze of the season blew through the park.

"You'd lose," Jack taunted.

"You'd lose," Ava taunted back. Every Saturday they met at the park in their neighborhood to shoot hoops.

Ava lined up her next shot. *Swish!* Jack shot from the corner. *Swish!*

They never played seriously, and they never talked much. The time they spent together was all about basketball and dreams of NBA glory.

Ava dribbled the ball from hand to hand, then ran in for the layup. *Bam!*

"Hey!" Jack cried, as a boy on a bike pedaled at top speed into the park. The bike skidded to a stop on the basketball court. "What's your deal, Corey?"

Corey's face was nearly as red as his hair. He breathed hard, but that seemed less from exercise and more from anger. "Valdeavano, what is with your cousin?"

"Lindsey?" Jack asked.

"Yeah, Lindsey." Corey gritted his teeth. "Have you seen the crazy web page she posted?"

Jack shook his head and looked to Ava. Ava shook her head too.

"Well, don't look when you get home," Corey said. "It's humiliating."

"What is it?" Ava asked tentatively.

"All these sickly sweet photos of us. Zillions of them. And all our friends on Buddybook got it!" Corey ranted.

"Why did she send it to everyone?" Jack asked.

"Good question!" Corey reached for the basketball and hurled it toward the hoop. He missed. "Actually, she says it's your sister's fault."

"What did Alex do?" Ava asked.

"Lindsey says she only meant to send it to me, which is creepy enough." He shook his head. "She said she sent it to Alex to show it to her for some reason, and she tagged Alex by mistake and then it went out everywhere. Why would your sister want pictures of us?"

"Maybe Alex *likes* you," Jack teased.

"Maybe Alex is friends with Lindsey," Ava countered. Boys could be such dopes. "Why doesn't Lindsey just ask Alex to take it down?"

"She's been trying to reach her." Corey blew out a big breath. "I'm done."

"Done with what?" Jack began shooting baskets again.

"Lindsey. I'm going to break up with her," Corey said.

"Just because she posted some photos?" Ava asked, incredulous. "You two are the perfect couple. Everyone says so."

"But we're not." Corey kicked at the pavement with his sneaker.

"For real?" Jack asked.

"Lindz and I have been friends since we were babies. She's cool. Or usually she is. But I'm not into her. She thinks she's not acting like a good enough girlfriend or something, but that's not it. I like her . . . just not that intensely."

"You could try," Ava suggested. She had no idea if this was the right thing to say. She'd never really had a boyfriend.

"I did. Besides, I like someone else," Corey said.

"Who?" Jack demanded.

"None of your business." Corey turned to Ava. "How do I break up with her?"

"Why are you asking me?" Ava shot the ball. It flew wide.

"Because you're a girl."

"That's my qualification?" Ava snorted.

"But you're cool like a guy. What do I say? I'm going to text her. Hey, you can help me write it now." Corey pulled out his phone.

"Wait a second, Corey." Ava rested the ball on the ground. "First, you cannot break up with her by text. That is so cowardly and cold. Second, I am not helping you break up with Lindsey. She and I are friends too."

"But we're better friends. You're one of the guys, so you have to be on my side," Corey pointed out.

"I didn't know there were sides," Ava said.

"Fine, then there aren't." Corey looked straight at her. "Just help me. I don't know what I'm doing here."

"And Ava does?" Jack laughed.

"He's right for once," Ava said, kicking the ball at Jack. "We should ask Alex to help. She's good at this kind of stuff."

"No way!" cried Corey. "Look, Ava, if *you* don't help me, I'm going to text her and she'll be mad and that'll be bad."

Ava sighed. "Okay, here's what I think. You tell Lindsey in person. Haven't your families been friends since forever? I think you owe her that much. And just tell her the truth. Tell her that you guys work better as friends."

"And tell her you like another girl," Jack put in.

Ava glared at Jack. "Do *not* tell her that, Corey." She knew very little about boyfriends and girlfriends, but she knew no girl wanted to be cast aside for another girl. For a moment, she wondered about the identity of this mystery girl. Could it be Alex? Her twin had once liked Corey . . . and it seemed like he had liked her, too. She shook her head. That was a while ago. Maybe Charlotte? She decided that she didn't care.

"Excellent!" Corey clapped his hands together. "You guys want to play H-O-R-S-E?"

"Don't you have to go break up with your girlfriend?" Jack asked.

"Not now. I'll do it later." Corey pointed at Ava. "Don't tell anyone."

"I won't," Ava promised. But it wasn't going to be easy keeping this news from Alex.

CHAPTER EIGHT

Ava brushed Chester's dark mane with long strokes. "You like having your hair brushed, don't you?" she whispered into the horse's ear.

Chester was too busy swatting flies with his tail to answer.

"Well, I like it," Ava said, patting his strong neck. "Grooming you is fun."

"Yeah, when you get to do the brushing part," Kylie McClaire said as she chipped the mud from Chester's hooves with a hoof pick.

"But you brush Chester every day." Ava scratched Kylie's horse behind his brown, velvety ear. "You're so lucky that you get to groom all these horses." Ava swept her arm in the direction of the six horses standing in stalls in the large barn.

"But I also have to rake hay and shovel manure," Kylie reminded her. Kylie had become Ava's closest *girl* friend in Ashland. Kylie was so unlike Lindsey and Emily and the rest of the girls who hung out with Alex. She wasn't into football or cheerleading. Kylie lived on a ranch on the outskirts of town, and every day after school she was expected to help, even though her family employed two ranch hands, Jorge and Luciana.

Like Ava, Kylie wasn't afraid to get dirty. With her dozens of little braids and her off-beat fashion sense, Kylie stood apart from the girls at school, but she didn't seem to care. She loved fantasy fiction and competed in junior rodeos. Ava had never been around horses until she met Kylie, but now she looked forward to spending a day in the McClaires' barn.

"Now that football's over, you can come here after school and Luciana can give you riding lessons," Kylie offered. "By this time next year, you'll be good enough to do a mini rodeo."

"I probably won't be here next year." Ava stopped brushing. She figured they'd stay in Ashland until the end of the school year, but what if they had to leave right away? What if the Tigers lost the game and everyone was so angry that her family was forced out of town? Her body swayed uneasily as she pondered this horrible reality.

"What are you talking about?" Kylie demanded.

Ava explained about Coach's one-year contract. Then she told Kylie about her failed attempt with Mr. Whittaker.

"You can't go!" Kylie cried.

"I know," Ava agreed. "But how do I make sure we stay?"

Kylie sat back on her heels and thought. "Your dad's job made you move to Ashland, so if you want to stay, your dad needs a job in Ashland. He doesn't have to be a coach, does he?"

"I don't know," Ava said. "All he's ever been is a coach. His whole life has been about football."

"He could run a sports store," Kylie suggested.

"Ashland already has Rico's Sports." Ava thought some more as she began to braid Chester's mane. "He likes to bake, too."

"How about that cupcake store in the mall?" Kylie asked.

"That's barely a store. It's more like a hut with one teenage girl selling cupcakes." Ava could not see Coach, with his broad shoulders, squeezed in there all day. Besides, he hated the noise of the mall. "No, I guess he has to keep being a football coach."

"What about your mom?" Kylie asked. "It doesn't have to be your dad. If your mom gets a great job in Ashland, then you can stay here."

"My mom has a job, remember? She started her ceramics business. She's been selling those blue-glazed pots."

"That's a problem. If you guys move, her job goes with you," Kylie pointed out.

"You're not helping!" Ava protested.

"Your mom needs a new job that can only be done here in Ashland." Kylie led Chester into his stall and closed the door. "I have an idea. Follow me!"

Ava followed Kylie into the tack room. Worn leather saddles and bridles hung from hooks on the wall. Kylie picked up a folded newspaper from beside a basket filled with canvas work gloves. "Jorge always reads the *Ashland Times*."

Kylie opened the newspaper to the help wanted ads. "We'll find your mom a job in here."

"But I don't know that she wants another job," Ava said.

"She will if we find her the perfect one. Her

fantasy job!" Kylie ran her finger down the list as she read aloud the choices. "Dishwasher? Receptionist? Housekeeper?"

Ava shook her head. "Why would she want to give up ceramics to wash dishes? She hates washing dishes."

"She doesn't have to give up making ceramics. She just needs a second job in Ashland," Kylie explained. "There are more here. Home aide for an elderly man? Plumber's assistant?"

"Do you really think unclogging toilets is my mom's *fantasy* job?" Ava cried, looking over Kylie's shoulder. "All these jobs are lame. Wait. What's this one?"

"'Elementary school art teacher,'" Kylie read. "The position is a replacement for a teacher who is leaving to have a baby. The ad says 'potential for permanent employment.' That means if they like her, they'll give her a job forever. How great would that be?"

"My mom loves art, and she used to be an elementary school teacher when we lived in Massachusetts," Ava said. "It's the perfect combination."

"It's more than perfect. Look at the name of the school. Rosewood Academy!" Kylie cried.

"Is that the small private school with the red-tiled roof?" Ava asked.

"Exactly! And the principal, Mrs. Cookson, lives right down the road. Let's go talk to her now." Kylie tucked the newspaper under her arm and headed out of the barn.

"Hold up." Ava ran after her. "I admire your can-do attitude—I haven't seen a lot of that lately at my house—but don't you think I should ask my mom first?"

"Wouldn't it be so much cooler if you could go home and tell your mom that you already got her the job?" Kylie asked. She pointed to two bikes leaning against the side of the garage. "Mrs. Cookson is really nice."

Ava imagined her family's faces when she announced that she'd solved their problem all on her own—and with a job that was perfect for her mom. If she did it now, Coach could relax about the big game. Winning would still be important, but the outcome wouldn't decide her family's future.

Ava and Kylie pedaled single file down the long dirt road that ran alongside the ranch. Few cars traveled on this road. The flat farmland stretched for miles under the huge blue Texas sky. Around a sharp bend, a small stucco house on a slight hill came into view. As they walked their bikes along a winding path bordered by cactus, Ava told Kylie about Corey and Lindsey.

"I promised him that I wouldn't tell anyone," Ava confessed. But the secret had been bothering her. And not sharing it with Alex felt wrong.

"Who am I going to tell?" Kylie asked. "I'm not close with those girls."

"Yeah." Ava had already considered this.

"This breakup is going to be huge. Everyone at school's going to be talking about it. Are you going to warn Lindsey?" Kylie asked.

Ava shook her head. "I don't want to be involved. Besides, Corey and I are friends."

"You're taking Corey's side. That makes you involved," Kylie pointed out.

"I'm not taking anyone's side," Ava insisted. A tall young woman rounded the house as they approached.

"Hello there!" she called in a husky voice. She wore a flowing white tunic embroidered with tiny flowers over a long skirt. Her light-brown hair hung down her back in a braid, and she carried a basket filled with large, ruffled green leaves. "Kylie, what a nice surprise. I just picked the last of the spinach from my garden. You can bring some home for your family."

"Thanks, Mrs. Cookson." Kylie introduced Ava.

How can this woman be a school principal? Ava wondered. All the principals she'd ever met had been much older, and they wore boring, sensible suits and shoes. She glanced down at Mrs. Cookson's blue-polished toenails peeking out from her sandals. *Her school must be cool,* Ava decided. Her mom would like that.

As Mrs. Cookson led them inside her cozy house, Kylie explained that Ava's mom was looking for a job as an art teacher. Ava wasn't sure this was exactly true, but she didn't want to tell a stranger that her dad might be fired. Mrs. Cookson didn't make the Sackett connection, which was good. Ava doubted she was interested in football. Her kitchen was filled with Zen sayings and crystals.

Ava told her everything she could think of about her mom. "She's the most amazing artist. She can draw and paint. She's super creative and has lots of energy. She used to teach in Boston. We moved to Ashland about four months ago."

"Really?" Mrs. Cookson turned to her with interest. "So she has a teaching degree?"

"She does. It's framed in our house. Little kids *love* her." Ava emphasized this important fact.

"Why didn't she get a teaching job when she moved?" Mrs. Cookson began to rinse the spinach leaves in the sink.

"She wanted to try starting a ceramics business. She's gotten tons of orders," Ava said proudly. The interview was going better than she'd expected. Then she noticed a laptop on the counter. "Do you want to see her website?"

Mrs. Cookson nodded, and Ava went over to the laptop and started typing. Her mom's home page appeared on the screen. *Laura Sackett Ceramics* flashed in a brilliant blue type that matched the color of her mother's pots in the picture below.

"She looks like you," Mrs. Cookson commented, drying her hands on a dish towel. Then she oohed and aahed over the photos of the ceramics. The famous blue-glazed bowls. Ombré pots in a sunset palette. Stone-baked canisters with whimsical handles.

"I would certainly like to meet your very talented mom," Mrs. Cookson said. "I'm in quite a bind. Our teacher had to leave earlier than we'd expected. Her doctor put her on bed rest, because she's having twins."

"I'm a twin," Ava offered. *Would that help?* she wondered.

"Fabulous. Your mom will understand my situation." Mrs. Cookson regarded Kylie, then Ava. "She is interested in this job, correct?"

"Totally!" Kylie said before Ava had the chance. "Will you hire her?"

Mrs. Cookson chuckled. "Let's start with an interview." She clicked open her calendar on the computer. "This week is crazy. How about she comes to talk to me at the school a week from tomorrow?"

"Perfect! Thank you!" Ava said. The timing couldn't be better. Friday was the big game in Austin. They'd spend Saturday in the city and drive home on Sunday. On Monday her mom would nail down the new job.

Mrs. Cookson hugged Kylie good-bye. Ava reached out her hand, and they shook on the deal. Then Mrs. Cookson hugged her, too!

Kylie and Ava walked their bikes back down the path. Kylie held a brown bag filled with spinach. As soon as they reached the dirt road, Ava pedaled fast, enjoying the sweet Texas sunshine on her face. She waved to a cow in the field and let out a *whoop!*

"I'm staying in Ashland!" she cried.

CHAPTER NINE

Are you sure?

Alex stared at Lindsey's latest text. Alex had promised her over and over. She'd even shown her proof online. What more did Lindsey need?

100% sure it's totally gone.

She'd deleted the online scrapbook from her page yesterday, as soon as she noticed Lindsey's frantic texts.

I should've tried harder to steer Lindsey away from the whole scrapbook idea, Alex thought. She felt guilty, even though Ava kept reminding her that Lindsey had been the one to mistakenly send it out. But still, *she* had designed the scrapbook.

One more example of how I mess everything up, Alex thought.

She'd spent the entire day on the sofa, watching Spanish soap operas. She didn't even speak Spanish! Her mom thought she was being industrious and teaching herself Spanish. That would have been typical of the old Alex. But new Alex stared at the television, not caring that she didn't understand anything.

I can't study right, spell right, run a bake sale, or give my friend decent boy advice, she thought. She knew she was having a pity party, but she felt she deserved one. A big one. How could she ever hope to run a big company or even be the mayor of Ashland? Lindsey texted again.

Corey is coming over tonight.

Alex glanced at the clock in the family room.

Eight o'clock on a Sunday night. That seemed like an odd time for him to come over, but what did she know? Maybe boyfriends stopped by on Sunday nights. She looked across the room at her dad frantically typing on his phone. Ava and her mom sat side by side on the sofa watching a cooking competition on TV, where the contestants created a dessert using cauliflower and chocolate. Tommy was doing his homework in the kitchen and drumming on the table.

Tonight would probably not be a good night for a boyfriend to stop by here, Alex thought.

Not that it was a possibility.

"Just great, just great," her dad muttered. He tucked his phone in the pocket of his shorts and paced in front of the television.

"Michael, what's wrong?" Mrs. Sackett lowered the volume with the remote control.

"PJ Kelly." He scratched his head in disbelief. "My star quarterback has the flu."

"What?" Ava cried, leaping up from the sofa.

"Are you sure?" Mrs. Sackett asked.

"I don't know, Laura, I'm not a doctor," her dad snapped. He rarely snapped at them. Alex could tell he was very upset.

"But did a doctor say PJ is sick?" Ava asked.

The noise in the kitchen stopped. Alex suspected Tommy was listening in.

Coach blew out his breath. "He's sick. Maybe it's the flu. Maybe it's a virus. Doesn't matter what you call it. The boy is in bed with a fever, sore throat, and snot pouring out of his nose."

"It's Sunday. The game isn't until Friday," Mrs. Sackett reminded him. "PJ could easily get better by then."

"Totally," Alex chimed in. As bad as she felt, she hated to see her dad so distraught.

"He could. Or he could not." Her dad rubbed his temples with his fingers. "PJ won't be at practice all week, and Dion's sidelined. We'll have to run the plays with Tom."

"That's so great for Tommy!" Ava said, then noticed their dad's scowl. "I mean, not that the first-string quarterback is sick." As she reconsidered the situation, her face changed. Anxiety replaced her initial joy for their brother. "Actually, this is kind of bad. Having only one healthy quarterback. For the team winning and all."

Alex heard the back door creak as it opened and closed.

"Tom doesn't even know all the plays." Coach Sackett paced faster. His voice grew louder.

"We're going to have to review the playbook page by page."

"I can help," Ava offered.

"Tom! Tom!" their dad yelled. "Tom, get out here!"

"Tommy learns stuff like this fast," Ava promised.

"Where is he?" Coach Sackett demanded when Tommy didn't answer or appear.

"I think he went out," Alex offered.

"What? Out? Where would he go on a Sunday night?" her dad asked, poking his head into the empty kitchen.

"To see his girlfriend?" Alex guessed. Tommy must have gone to Cassie's house to escape Coach's football flip-out. Alex didn't blame him. Maybe that's why Corey was heading to Lindsey's house now. Maybe he needed someone to talk to.

Coach Sackett hurried to the back door. "Well, I'm getting him back here. This is serious! We have major work to do."

"Not now." Mrs. Sackett scrambled off the sofa and ran after him. "Let Tom see Cassie for an hour or so. He needs time to get used to this idea—"

"We don't have time," interrupted her dad.

"Yes, you do. Tom will learn the plays. He

wasn't expecting this." She spoke in a soothing voice. She gently turned him away from the door and simultaneously pulled his phone from his pocket. "How about you take a minute to decompress too and scoop ice cream for all of us? There's a quart of cookies and cream in the freezer."

"Fine," he grumbled.

Mrs. Sackett returned to the family room. "Alex," she hissed. "Disable the computer."

"What?" Alex said.

"Do something so your dad cannot see all the chatter once Ashland discovers PJ is ill. He needs a break tonight. We all do. I have his phone." She held it up. "You're our family techie. Do something to the computer. Fast!"

Alex ran through the possibilities as she walked over to the computer. Unplugging it wouldn't do much. The computer would still have power. Her eye caught a blog post right before she closed out all the open screens and slid the battery from the computer. She handed the battery to Ava, who tucked it under a sofa cushion just as Coach arrived with the bowls of ice cream.

"What was that blog post about your ceramics?" Alex tried to direct the conversation away from PJ and Tommy.

Mrs. Sackett beamed. "A blogger from the Texas Arts Council raved about my pots. He called me the newest Texas talent."

"That's amazing, Laura. Let's toast your mom." Coach raised his spoon. Ava and Alex did the same.

"Thanks. I'm so happy I finally had the courage to open my ceramics business. If we hadn't moved, I would've kept putting it off," she said.

"But you were happy when you were a teacher," Ava protested.

"Sure, but ceramics gives me creative joy that I never got while teaching. And there's nothing better than being my own boss," she said.

"You don't have to give up teaching," Ava said. "What if you combined ceramics and teaching?"

Alex tilted her head. What was Ava getting at?

"Oh, Ave, do you mean that you want to learn? I'd love to teach *you* how to throw pots on the wheel." Their mom's eyes brightened at the prospect. Alex had refused her offer long ago. Clay was so messy.

"No, I don't want to learn." Ava stirred her ice cream vigorously until it melted into soup. Alex couldn't understand why her twin looked so disappointed.

911!!! Call me!!! Now!!!

The text from Lindsey flashed on the screen of Alex's phone.

"I'm going up to my room," Alex said, standing.

"Bring your bowl to the sink. And Alex, a shower might be a good idea," her mom suggested. "Freshen up for school tomorrow?"

"This is a first for Alex," Ava quipped. "I can't believe it, but your hair is looking gnarly."

"Whatever." Alex no longer cared how she looked for school.

In the privacy of her room, Alex called Lindsey. At first she heard only strange, hiccuping sobs. "Lindsey? Lindsey, is that you? What's wrong?"

"He—he—he—" Lindsey sputtered, then sobbed.

"He what?" Alex demanded. "Corey? Are you talking about Corey?"

"Yes." Lindsay gulped, as if she couldn't suck in enough air. "He broke up with me."

"He what? No, he didn't." This was ludicrous. Corey wouldn't break up with Lindsey.

"He did." Lindsey hiccuped, fighting to control her tears.

"But you just threw him a party. And you made that scrapbook with all those cute photos to show him how much you like him," Alex protested.

"I know. That's why." Lindsey sobbed softly. "He blamed all that. That and other things. He said I text too much. That I'm too intense. I'm not intense, am I?"

"Of course not," Alex said soothingly. Although she was. Kind of. But not in a bad way.

"He said all the photos in the scrapbook embarrassed him. That it was way over the top."

Alex picked at her nail polish. *That was my idea,* she thought, feeling enormously guilty. "I can talk to him for you. Tell him it was my idea and apologize or . . ." Alex wasn't quite sure what she'd say.

"No, it's not your fault." Lindsey had stopped crying. "I really like him. I thought he'd want to know that, you know?"

Alex flopped on her bed. "I'm so sorry, Lindz." She could feel her friend's pain through the phone. And despite what Lindsey said, the scrapbook and the party *had* been her fault. She could fix the spelling mistake on the banner. She could live with the stupid Variety Show theme. She could even, sort of, deal with the horrible grades. But she had no idea how to make her friend feel better.

And that, more than anything, made her feel completely useless.

"So what did she say?" Kylie asked Ava during lunch on Monday.

Ava glanced next to Kylie at Nicole Patel. Nicole sat with her back toward Ava. Her hands waved as she told her own friends a story. She didn't care what Ava and Kylie had to say.

When they'd entered the cafeteria, Ava had immediately spotted Alex and Emily huddled around Lindsey at the table where they all often sat. Corey, Logan, Jack, and Owen, who Kylie was sort of going out with, had retreated to the other half of the table. Corey had waved Ava over.

Ava knew about the breakup. The whole school knew about the breakup.

Ava could not deal with more drama. She'd grabbed Kylie's hand. "Let's sit over there today," she'd suggested. They'd found seats at the end of a table populated by girls in the drama club.

Now Ava inspected her apple for bruises. She hated the brown spots. "I didn't tell her."

"Why not?" Kylie demanded.

"My mom started going on about how much she loves her ceramics." Ava bit into the apple and chewed slowly. "I'm worried that the teaching thing isn't going to work."

"Maybe the Tigers will win," Kylie offered.

Ava rolled her eyes. She told Kylie about PJ's sickness. "Our staying in Ashland now rests on Tommy's quarterback abilities."

"I thought Tommy was good," Kylie said.

"He is, but his confidence is shaky. I don't know if Coach sees it, but Tommy's not totally committed to football. He's so into his music."

"Why can't he be into both?" Kylie asked.

"He can. But Coach demands one hundred and ten percent commitment. I think sometimes that messes with Tommy's mind, and he doubts how good he is," Ava said. "So, basically, I need to start packing my bags."

"Don't say that!" Kylie cried. "The job at Rosewood could still happen, or we'll think of something else."

"Lindsey, wait!" Alex's voice carried across the cafeteria.

Ava swiveled to see Lindsey stalking toward them. Alex hurried after her, and the rest of the cheerleaders trailed behind them. Conversation throughout the cafeteria stopped. All eyes tracked Lindsey.

"How could you? How could you?" Lindsey demanded, now standing alongside Ava.

"What are you talking about?" Ava looked to Alex for a clue.

Alex stared at the ceiling with that overwhelmed expression she'd worn for the past few days.

"You told Corey to break up with me," Lindsey stated flatly.

"What? No, I didn't!" Ava cried. "Corey told you *that*?"

"He didn't have to. Jack told Bryce, who told Annelise. I heard that you even told him what to say. Why would you do this?" Lindsey asked angrily.

"That wasn't what happened," Ava said. "Corey told me on Saturday that he was going to end things, but—"

"*Saturday?*" Lindsey shrieked. "You knew then and never told me?"

"Or me," Alex added so quietly that only Ava heard.

Ava shot her twin a guilty look, then turned

to Lindsey. "He swore me to secrecy. I tried to talk to him about it. I really did."

"I don't get why *you* were giving advice to Lindsey's boyfriend," Emily put in.

"I wasn't. I only told him to do it nicely," Ava explained. She felt as if she were on trial. "I'm friends with both of you."

"If you were really my friend, shouldn't you be telling him *not* to do it?" Lindsey demanded. "Or did you want him to break up with me? Maybe this was your idea."

"It had nothing to do with me." Ava felt that fluttery, nervous sensation she got before a test. She never felt comfortable on the spot in front of big groups of girls. She searched the cafeteria for Corey. He and the other guys had fled. She wished she could go too.

"It's like you were plotting against me," Lindsey said.

"I wasn't." Ava didn't know how to make Lindsey believe her.

"Why did he do it? Tell me what he said," Lindsey prodded.

"I don't want to talk about it," Ava said. Kylie gently grabbed her elbow and tried to get her to stand up so they could leave.

"You're trying to protect your football buddy," Lindsey accused.

"No, I'm not," Ava insisted. "It wasn't like the breakup was all of a sudden. He mentioned it once before—"

"And you never told me?" Lindsey cried.

At that moment, the bell rang. Ava had never been so happy to escape to English class. She grabbed her lunch bag and notebooks and edged herself around Lindsey. "I'm sorry," she said sincerely. Then she walked away.

Alex caught up. "What are you sorry for?"

"I don't know. I guess that she's sad, because Corey broke up with her," Ava said. "I didn't do anything wrong. Corey didn't either, really."

"I don't get how you can side with him," Alex said.

"I don't want to be involved," Ava said.

"But you are. I am too." Alex stopped in the middle of the crowded hall. "I'm on Lindsey's side. Are you with us?"

"No," Ava said. "I'm not taking sides."

CHAPTER TEN

Alex kept waiting for things to turn around. She thought maybe on Tuesday, when she got an A on her science lab, the old Alex was back. Then, when she'd been working on her social studies paper on her laptop, she'd forgotten to hit save, and as she switched screens to look up a fact, the entire paper disappeared. *Poof!* All that work, for nothing.

Lindsey joined her, walking around school in a funk. The girls and boys in their group weren't speaking, each side blaming the other for how the breakup went down. Alex felt the tension Lindsey and Corey had created. *Ava and I helped create it too,* she thought.

She was angry with Ava for not telling her about Corey's feelings. If she had, Alex would never have made that scrapbook. Then Lindsey would never have messed up sending it out, and Corey wouldn't have gotten angry and maybe they'd still be together.

Ava kept trying not to take sides, and as a result both the girls and now the boys were annoyed with her. She had been sticking with Kylie, and she and Alex hadn't spoken much.

On Wednesday, Mrs. Sackett had left instructions for Alex and Ava to bake the frozen lasagna she'd made because she had to go out to help the Booster Club assemble boxed dinners for the team to eat on the bus ride to Austin. Alex read the handwritten instructions, then set the note aside without turning on the oven. Why bother? She was sure to mess up even something as simple as sliding the pan into the oven. Ava didn't bother either.

Their mom was angry, but she seemed to forget about it as she rushed to pack everyone for Austin. All week Coach and Tommy had been at the field, practicing for the game. Mrs. Sackett had been busy with a new order of blue-glazed pots after her blog fame. They ended up ordering pizza. No one noticed that a gray cloud had settled over the Sackett twins.

"Everyone ready?" Mrs. Sackett asked on Thursday afternoon. "How fun will this be? The big game? And traveling to Austin? And staying in a hotel with all your friends?"

"Great," Alex said halfheartedly, trying to show the excitement that everyone around her felt.

The marching band paraded through the high school parking lot, blasting a syncopated rendition of "Eye of the Tiger." The dance team followed in high-kicking rows, their orange-and-blue sequined leotards glittering in the sun. The cheerleaders, who'd painted their faces to resemble fierce tigers, led the crowd in a wild roar. Hundreds of people, young and old, had come out to see the team off.

Alex spotted the middle school banner and sighed with relief. GO ASHLAND TIGERS! The typo had been fixed, and Mrs. Gusman hadn't asked her to pay.

The entire football team, plus coaches and trainers and Mr. Whittaker, piled onto two yellow school buses painted with black tiger stripes. They'd been scheduled to depart thirty minutes ago, but the festivities had run long.

"There's Tommy," she said when she spotted their brother's face in one of the front windows.

"Hey, look." Ava pointed to a window several rows back. "Is that PJ Kelly? Is he playing?"

"You know it, Sackett!" Andy Baker pushed in beside them. He stood with his parents and the entire Kelly family, who seemed to have brought dozens of blond-haired cousins. "PJ is QB number one. He's tough. He beat back that cold, and he's going to beat back the Crawford Colts. You can tell your bro to get comfy on the bench. State will be the PJ Show!"

"Andy!" Mrs. Kelly said. She turned to Mrs. Sackett and smiled sweetly. "My nephew didn't mean that."

Ava gritted her teeth and gave Alex a sideways glance. Andy *definitely* meant that. Alex had hoped PJ would get better so Tommy didn't have to play. She knew how nervous he was. Now she wanted her big brother on the field to show up Andy's cousin big-time.

"State! State! State!" Someone by the buses started the chant, and the entire crowd joined in. Alex found herself joining in as her dad shook

Mayor Johnston's hand and waved to all the supporters.

"Do you think he's going to make a speech?" Alex asked Ava.

"Nah. Coach saves his speeches for the locker room," Ava said. "Look! They're going!"

The buses beeped their horns and began to inch forward. Cheerleaders, dancers, and the marching band members scattered to various corners of the parking lot to board their own buses. Families retreated to their cars to follow the different buses on the three-hour journey to Austin.

"Hurry, girls." Mrs. Sackett led them to their red SUV. Ava had scrawled TIGERS RULE on the side windows with white paint marker.

Alex and Ava both opened the back doors.

"No one wants to sit up front with me?" Mrs. Sackett tucked her long brown hair behind her ears.

Alex looked at Ava. Ava shrugged. "Not so much," they both said at the same time.

"You usually fight to sit in the front. What's going on? Oh, the bus is moving! Close the doors and buckle up," she instructed, sliding in behind the wheel. "I need to keep the bus in sight. I'm a bit iffy on the directions, so I don't want to lose sight of them."

Alex staked out her side of the backseat. She popped in her earbuds. She glanced over at Ava. Her sister had done the same. An invisible line was drawn between them.

At least we don't have to squeeze back here with Moxy, Alex thought. They'd left their dog with Kylie's dad, who was staying home. Moxy loved to run around the ranch.

Alex watched her mom pull out behind the tiger-striped bus and head down the road that led out of Ashland. Alex chewed her bottom lip. Should she offer to navigate? Her mother said she was better at it than their GPS app, but surely she'd mess it up. Messing up seemed to be her new thing. Instead she turned up the volume of the next song.

They traveled through Texas farmland, keeping mostly to rural back roads. The bus stayed directly in front of them. Many parents sped ahead of the slow buses, eager to reach Austin. Only a few followed behind. After an hour, Ava dozed off. Mrs. Sackett sang along to the country radio station. Alex slipped out one earbud to listen. Her mom's deep voice brought more warmth to the song than the singer who'd made it famous.

"You could do that," Alex said.

"Do what?" Mrs. Sackett asked, still humming.

"Sing on the radio. Don't you want to?" Alex asked.

Mrs. Sackett chuckled. "I used to. When I was your age, I dreamed of singing in front of a huge audience."

"So?" Alex demanded.

"So what?" Her mom shrugged. "Sometimes dreams don't happen. I got sidetracked, I guess, and gave up on it. But I sing now with the church choir, and I have my art."

"But did you ever *try*?" Alex asked.

Mrs. Sackett shook her head. "I probably wasn't good enough . . . oh!"

They both heard a *thump!* Then a rattle.

"What's that?" Alex cried.

Her mom struggled with the steering wheel. The car wobbled, then jerked to the left. They bumped onto the shoulder of the road. Her foot slammed on the brakes.

"Hey!" Ava jolted awake.

Their mom turned off the car and sighed. "I think we just got a flat tire."

Alex reached for her door handle.

"No! Don't get out. You'll get hit by another car!" Mrs. Sackett cried. She clicked on the hazard lights.

Alex gazed at the surrounding farmland. The cars traveling behind hadn't yet reached them. *I'd sooner get run down by one of the brown cows far off in the field than a car,* she thought. But since Mrs. Sackett's brow had wrinkled with a worried look, she stayed put.

"I'm calling Coach." Ava lifted her phone and quickly spoke to their dad.

Alex watched out the front window as the bus backed up, then stopped. Her dad stepped out and jogged a few feet down the side of the road. With his hand, he kept his orange baseball cap from flying off his head in the breeze. Mrs. Sackett met him, and together they surveyed the back left tire.

"How much longer to Austin?" Ava asked Alex.

Alex quickly calculated the distance. "Maybe a little less than two hours?"

"How long does it take to change a tire?" Ava asked.

"Beats me. I've never done that. Why?" Alex asked.

"The team has a practice in the Austin stadium at seven o'clock tonight. It's their only practice on the field before the game tomorrow. They can't miss it," Ava said.

Alex did the math. Even without changing the tire, getting to the stadium would be tight.

The trunk popped open. "Hey, girls." Their dad grinned in at them. Then he stepped back, as he took in all the suitcases, comforters, pillows, and stuffed animals that crowded the space. "What's with all this? Hotels have bedding."

"I like my flannel comforter, Coach. You know that," Ava said. She hated rough blankets.

"And I can't sleep without my own pillow," Alex said.

"And without Poppet," Ava added.

Alex reached over the seat and snatched her bedraggled, barely stuffed rabbit. She'd slept with Poppet forever. Going to bed without her pale-pink bunny felt wrong.

"Scoot out and help me unload this stuff. I need to unearth the spare tire and a jack." Coach began piling their bags behind the car.

Alex stepped into the slightly cool air. The sky showed hints of purple. The sun would soon set. The high school boys pressed their faces against the back windows of the bus. She felt ridiculous holding Poppet under her arm. *They must think I'm a silly little kid,* she thought.

She perched Poppet on top of the suitcases

and comforters that created a wall around the back of the car. She watched her dad pry the silver hubcap off the tire.

Her phone buzzed. Tommy texted.

Are you guys OK? Driver won't let me off bus. School rules.

Flat tire.

Alex planned to write more, but then she heard Mr. Whittaker.

"Mike! Mike! What is going on?" Mr. Whittaker, his belly straining against a too-tight Ashland High sweatshirt, hurried off the bus and down the road toward them.

"Flat tire, Floyd," Mrs. Sackett explained.

"Listen, darlin', I'm sorry about that. Tough break, but you've got a spare, so you'll be fine. Mike, we need you back on the bus," Mr. Whittaker said.

"I don't know how to change a tire," their mom admitted. "I'm sorry, Floyd."

"Laura, some other fine person will help you. Aha! Here comes the cavalry!" Two other cars pulled up several feet behind them.

"See?" Mr. Whittaker said. "Now, come back on the bus, Mike."

"Give me a minute." Coach Sackett strained to loosen the lug nuts with the wrench.

"There's no time. We need to get moving, or we will miss this practice." Mr. Whittaker's voice grew harder.

"I'm not leaving my family on the side of the road." Coach wedged the jack under the car. He pumped the handle to raise the car.

"You must get back on that bus. You are putting the team in jeopardy," Mr. Kelly said, getting out of one of the cars. Now he stood with Mr. Whittaker.

"All I'm asking for is a minute here," Coach growled. He stood and wiped his hands on his khaki shorts.

The football players began to pound on the windows. The bus appeared to shake.

"Mike, your job specifies that you are to be on that bus with those boys, not with your family," Mr. Whittaker said. "I'm speaking on behalf of the Booster Club."

"I agree." Another man had left his car and joined the adults. "I'm speaking on behalf of the school board."

"I can't leave until the tire's changed," Coach protested.

The adults moved, so they now stood on one side of the suitcase-comforter barrier. Alex and Ava remained on the other side with the spare tire and the tools.

"Just get on the bus and do your job!" cried Mr. Kelly. He lifted his cuff to show everyone the time on his watch.

"Do my job? In this town, it seems as if football coach is everyone's job." Coach threw his arms up in exasperation.

"What's that supposed to mean?" Mr. Whittaker countered.

"If you just step back and let him work, Michael will fix the tire *and* win the game," Mrs. Sackett said.

"Not if we get there too late to practice," the man on the school board grumbled. "This is not about what *you* want, Coach."

"This is bad," Ava murmured. "They'll never let us stay in Ashland now."

Alex watched the boys slide the bus windows

down to hear the argument. She watched the adults yelling about the time and coaching and who knew what else. She studied the tools at her feet and the car jacked up off the ground.

This is crazy, she thought. *The tire could've been changed by now.*

She clicked on her phone and found a step-by-step tire-changing video. Not too hard, she decided.

"Ava," Alex said. "Help me." She handed her sister her phone.

Ava glanced at the video. "But we don't know how. We could mess it up."

For a second, Alex wavered. Ava was right, they *could* mess it up. But then she heard the adults shouting. She remembered the time. She thought about the team not practicing and not winning, and her dad losing his job and her family leaving Ashland.

"We can't think like that. We should try." She grabbed the tire wrench. "I think I remove the lug nuts." Alex crouched next to the tire. "These look like lug nuts, right?"

Ava crouched next to her. She held the phone screen next to the tire, as if playing a matching game. "They have to be."

Alex twisted the wrench. The lug nuts popped off. She handed them one by one to Ava. Then, using both hands, she pulled off the tire. "Whoa!" She stumbled under its weight. None of the adults noticed. Their argument heated up. Mrs. Kelly joined her husband.

With Ava's help, Alex placed the flat tire on the ground next to the spare. "We're both going to have to lift the spare. On three," Alex commanded. "One . . . two . . . three." They hoisted the tire up and into place. Ava was strong from all that football conditioning.

Alex focused all her attention on the video. "Okay, now I need to put the lug nuts back on." Ava dropped the shiny pieces of metal into her sister's hand, and Alex tightened them into place. Then Alex instructed Ava how to use the jack to lower the car.

"This is fun," said Ava, pumping on the jack.

"It is, kind of," Alex agreed. She opened the trunk and put the flat tire where the spare used to be, then began to rearrange their stuff. She ordered it much better than their mom had. She tucked Poppet in beside her pillow.

As soon as their barrier disappeared, the

boys on the bus noticed the tire. They began to whistle and clap.

"What's going on?" Mr. Whittaker stopped arguing.

Alex waved the shiny hubcap over her head. "Excuse me!" she called. "If you don't want to miss that practice, everyone better start driving."

"But the tire? How?" Coach Sackett scratched his head as he walked toward the car.

"It's all changed." Alex handed him the wrench, and he checked that she'd properly tightened the lug nuts.

"Amazing!" he declared as he replaced the hubcap. "My twelve-year-old twins saved the day."

"It was Alex's idea," Ava said. She smiled warmly at her sister. The first time since the Lindsey-Corey argument.

"What a take-charge girl!" Mr. Whittaker patted her back. "Alex can do it all."

"No, I can't," Alex said. "I can't play football, and I can't drive that bus. Go, go, go!"

Because Mrs. Sackett had to drive more slowly on the spare tire, the Kellys agreed to stay near the Sacketts' car for the rest of the trip. Coach Sackett raced onto the bus with Mr. Whittaker. The players cheered, and the bus sped away.

"Alex is a dynamo!" Mrs. Kelly gushed to their mom.

As they settled back into the car, Ava sniggered. "You're a dynamo? Who says 'dynamo'?" she teased.

"Okay, maybe not the best word choice," Alex agreed. She smoothed her hair and sat up straighter. The old Alex was back!

No, not the old Alex, she decided after a minute. She wasn't perfect. She couldn't do everything all at once and do it well. *But that doesn't mean I can't get great grades and do great things,* she thought. *I'm not giving up on my dreams because of one bad week.*

She looked over the invisible line at Ava. She didn't know what was upsetting her twin more—the girls at school turning against her or the chance that Coach wouldn't be brought back next season. Alex suddenly wanted to fix everything for her.

One thing at a time, Alex cautioned herself. She'd let Tommy and the team work on winning the game. She'd find a way for their whole group to be friends again.

CHAPTER ELEVEN

Usually Ava hated noise and crowds, but not tonight. Sitting in the university stadium stands filled with Ashland orange and blue and hearing fans from all over root for the team her dad coached filled her with pride. She was a part of this too. A part of the town. A part of the team. In a strange way, she felt as if these strangers were rooting for her.

"Go Tigers!" she yelled spontaneously, as they walked down the bleachers to get in the concession stand line Friday night.

"Give 'em that roar, Sackett!" called a man she vaguely recognized from the car wash in their town.

And she did. She roared. A woman snapped her picture, and for once, Ava didn't care. Their team was ahead at halftime.

"Ave, do you want a soft pretzel or popcorn?" Alex asked when they reached the front of the line. Mrs. Sackett ordered three bottles of water.

"Pretzel." Ava spotted a woman with a long braid slung over one shoulder waving merrily at her. She raised her hand to wave back, then abruptly dropped it to her side. *What's* she *doing here?* she wondered. She'd never thought Mrs. Cookson would like football. She'd certainly never counted on her traveling to Austin for the game.

"Here." Alex pushed the warm pretzel into Ava's hand as they headed back to their seats. Oh no! In a matter of seconds, her mom and Mrs. Cookson would cross paths. She couldn't let that happen. Not now. Not yet. Mrs. Cookson would mention the interview on Monday, and Mrs. Sackett would be confused, and *ugh!* Ava groaned.

She'd planned to tell her mom before the game. Then they'd had the flat tire yesterday. When they'd arrived at the hotel, Mrs. Sackett helped settle all the football players, and then she and some of the other parents hosted a late-night coffee-and-cake party in the lobby. Today had been all about the game. They'd attended a pregame tailgate and had even been interviewed by two local newspapers and one local TV station.

And now the Tigers were ahead. *Maybe Mom won't have to go for the interview after all,* Ava figured. Then Ava remembered her own game. And her failed kick. Anything could happen in the second half.

"Mustard!" Ava cried. "I need mustard."

Alex wrinkled her nose. "Since when? You don't like mustard."

"I do now." She grabbed her mom's sleeve. "Mom, come to the condiments table with us." She expertly maneuvered her mom and sister away from Mrs. Cookson. The condiments table was crowded. Ava successfully tucked herself and her mom behind some large ex-football players drowning their fries in ketchup.

"Here's the mustard," Alex said, pointing to the large yellow jug.

"Oh." Ava contemplated squirting it on her pretzel. She was hungry, and the warm pretzel smelled so good. Why ruin it? "Actually, I've changed my mind."

"I knew it!" Alex said triumphantly. "You can't fool me."

"Hello, Ava. Enjoying the game?" Ava was startled to find Mrs. Cookson by her side. "This must be the twin sister you told me about."

"I'm Alex," Alex introduced herself before Ava could speak.

"Hi, I'm Michelle Cookson. Are you Laura Sackett?" She turned to their mom, who smiled back. Over the past day, Mrs. Sackett had become used to strangers coming up to her. Their whole family had gained instant celebrity.

"I am. Great game, isn't it? Both teams are playing so well," Mrs. Sackett replied, even though she had no idea who Mrs. Cookson was.

"I'm so glad we get to say hello now. I'm looking forward to hearing more about your ceramics," Mrs. Cookson said in her warm, husky voice.

"You are?" Mrs. Sackett smiled, but Ava could see her desperately trying to place the tall woman with the braid. She wore a white linen dress, which made her stand out among the fans in sports jerseys and logo sweatshirts.

"I'm curious to hear your thoughts on integrating ceramics into the existing arts curriculum.

In a private school, we are fortunate not to be restricted to certain mediums. There's a lot more freedom to experiment at Rosewood. It's what makes our school so special," Mrs. Cookson said.

"I'm sure it is, but, if you don't mind, who—" Mrs. Sackett began, obviously uncomfortable at not being able to follow the conversation.

"Oh, Mom. Mrs. Kelly is waving you over. She seems desperate to tell you something. Do you think it has to do with PJ? I hope he's feeling okay. He looked healthy in the first half, but you never know. You should go speak with her." The words tumbled out. Mrs. Kelly hadn't waved, but Ava had spotted her in the crowd. Ava didn't know how else to pull her mom away.

"Go, go, Laura. We'll have plenty of time to get to know each other later," Mrs. Cookson said graciously.

"Who was that?" Alex asked after they'd walked away.

"Truthfully, I have no idea." Mrs. Sackett shook her head. "I'm usually so good at remembering names and faces. This game must have rattled my brains. Or else I'm getting old and forgetful."

"You're not getting old," Ava assured her. "But

she seemed really nice. Didn't she?" She would fill her mom in later. After the game. After the Tigers won.

Please, please win, she sent a silent prayer to the football gods.

As the fourth quarter approached, Ava wasn't sure the football gods had heard. Or maybe they had and were mocking her. She should never have lied about Mrs. Kelly wanting to talk to her mom about PJ's health. The Tigers had maintained a slight lead throughout the entire game, but now PJ looked sluggish. His pace had slowed, and his passes lacked the speed and precision that had brought the team this far.

"PJ's not back to his full strength," Mrs. Sackett explained when Ava vented her frustration. The score was now tied.

"Well, he better do something. Someone better do something!" Ava cried. They were so close to winning. She couldn't imagine leaving Ashland because one boy hadn't been feeling well. Especially not if that boy was Andy's cousin!

She spotted the large Kelly/Baker family sitting a few sections away from them. Most of their friends who had traveled to the game sat with their families. Ava hadn't really spoken to anyone since arriving here. She and Alex had stayed in their room during the coffee-and-cake party, eating room service and watching a movie. At the tailgate, their family had been swarmed by well-wishers and reporters.

"Ave!" Alex grasped her arm and squeezed it. The fourth quarter was starting. "Dad is pulling PJ out. He's putting Tommy in!"

"Seriously?" Ava cried. Their mom began to cheer.

"Is this a good thing?" Alex asked.

"I'm not sure." Ava was nervous for Tommy. She couldn't see his face behind his helmet. She couldn't judge how confident he felt. "I want it to be a good thing."

Ava, Alex, and Mrs. Sackett balanced at the edge of their seats as Tommy threw pass after pass. They were solid passes, and the game slowly moved upfield.

"You can do this, Tommy!" Ava cheered until her voice was hoarse.

As time fell off the clock, Alex complained, "He's playing it too safe. He needs to do more!"

"No, he's playing it smart," Ava corrected. "He's keeping the game in our control." Slow and steady would let them win. Risky hero maneuvers could ruin it all. Ava trusted that Tommy knew that. *Of course he does,* she thought. Coach had trained him just as he'd trained her. Sacketts knew how to play football.

She glanced at Alex. Well, most Sacketts did.

With only two minutes left, the game remained tied. The crowd went wild. All eyes and hopes and dreams rested on Tommy. Tommy had successfully brought their team down to the thirty yard line, but Ava worried whether he could continue to stand up to the pressure. She feared going into overtime.

And then, as if he'd been reading her mind, Coach pulled Tommy out and sent PJ back into the game. The stands erupted at the sight of their beloved quarterback. PJ attacked with renewed energy. Tommy had allowed him to rest and had kept the game on track, setting up a great field position for his return.

Ava felt dizzy. In minutes the game would be over. Tommy might not have been the best player out there, but she knew he wanted to win for one of the same reasons she did—to stay in Ashland. Their fate now lay in the hands of Andy's cousin and Kylie's neighbor.

Thirty seconds after hitting the field, PJ

raced down the right side with the ball cradled in his arms. Linebackers cleared a path, blocking potential tackles. Ava sprang to her feet. "Go, go, go!" she screamed, as PJ ran past the twenty yard line . . . past the ten . . . the five . . . TOUCHDOWN!

The Tigers had won State!

Ava flung her arms around Alex. "We're staying!"

CHAPTER TWELVE

The lobby of their hotel felt like the middle of a parade in Ashland's town square. Everyone the Sacketts knew, and many people they didn't, crammed into the sleek space and offered hearty congratulations, backslaps, handshakes, and the majestic Tiger roar to the players and their families. Plans were made for celebration dinners and parties in Austin.

Ava waded through the crowd, then hesitated. Lindsey, Emily, Rosa, and several other girls from school sat on a black leather sofa along the lobby's far wall. Corey, Xander, Jack, Logan, and Andy bumped fists near a tall ficus tree by the reception desk. She didn't know where Alex had gone. She couldn't very well stand in the middle of this crowd by herself. Should she go over to the girls? Or the boys? What was she supposed to do? Now that Coach was assured a new contract—one that guaranteed his job for several years—Ava worried that this choice could define the rest of her life here in Ashland. Or at least, the rest of her time in middle school.

She spotted Coach and Tommy talking with the Kellys and Mr. Whittaker. She didn't feel like joining *that* conversation. Maybe her mom would hang out with her while she worked out what to do. Ava raised herself to her tiptoes to scan the sea of orange sweatshirts. Mrs. Cookson's white linen dress caught her attention. Ava sucked in her breath. Her mother stood with Mrs. Cookson! The two women appeared deep in conversation.

Not good. Not good at all, thought Ava, especially now that the team had won. *We didn't need a plan B. I never should have doubted Coach*, Ava chided herself.

Then Mrs. Cookson hugged her mom! What was *that* about?

Should I go over to them? Ava wondered, nervously shifting her weight. But her mom caught her eye and headed toward her. Ava stiffened.

"I've officially met Michelle Cookson," Mrs. Sackett said. Her voice didn't give anything away. Ava couldn't tell whether she should prepare for a scolding.

"She's nice, right? She likes to hug," Ava said, trying to sound neutral too.

"That she does. She told me what you did." Her mom's hazel eyes searched hers.

"I was only trying to help. Coach said he might not have a job if the team lost. But I *really* wanted to stay in Ashland, so I thought that if *you* had a job, we wouldn't have to move. Teaching and art together seemed like the perfect job. Please don't be mad. It doesn't matter now, anyway," Ava said.

"I'm touched, pumpkin. Quite impressed, actually," Mrs. Sackett said.

"Really?"

"Yes. You felt our family had a problem, and you took it upon yourself to find a solution. That takes a special kind of gumption." Her mom wrapped her arm around her. "I didn't know you were so scared about leaving here. You should've talked to me about that."

"Everyone was so busy with the football game.

I figured it would be better if I fixed it on my own." Ava grinned. "That's kind of an Alex thing, isn't it? Racing out and setting up a job interview?"

"Not anymore. Now it's an Ava thing too," Mrs. Sackett said. "But about the job . . . I told Mrs. Cookson I'm not interested in it."

Ava shrugged. "I figured that."

"But she invited me to be a part of the school's crafts fair. People come from all over. The fair should help get the word out about my ceramics business, so I have to thank you." Her mom paused, thinking. "And I really like Michelle. We have a lot of the same interests."

"So I found you a friend?" Ava asked. Her mom hadn't made many close friends yet in Ashland.

"I think you did." Her mom squeezed her tight. "Thank you for that. Oh, your dad is motioning me over. You should go have fun with *your* friends. Have everyone up to the room. Here's money for the vending machines. Just promise to stay in the hotel. We'll come check on you in a little bit."

Ava watched her mom join Coach. She looked again between the girls and the boys.

"What's wrong?" Alex asked, coming up behind her.

"I don't know which group I'm supposed to be with," Ava said.

"Well, I'm going to solve your problem: I'm going to get Lindsey and Corey back together," Alex announced.

"What makes you think you can do that?" Ava asked. "You know nothing about matchmaking."

"I knew nothing about changing a tire, and we did that," Alex countered.

"We had a video to talk us through it," Ava pointed out.

"Details!" Alex grabbed her hand. "Have some confidence. We can do this! Let's talk to Lindsey first."

Ava followed her sister over to the sofa. Before Alex could speak, Ava jumped in. "Lindsey, I'm sorry. I was trying to be a good friend to Corey, and I guess that made me a bad friend to you."

"No, I shouldn't have yelled like that," Lindsey admitted. "I was really upset on Monday. I'm *so* much better now."

"Better how?" Alex asked.

"Like I don't care about Corey. He got pushed into going out with me, because our parents are close. Deep down I always sensed that he wasn't into it. That's why I was trying so hard to make it right. But it's his loss. I was a great girlfriend," Lindsey boasted.

"You were," Alex agreed, and the other girls backed her up.

"Besides"—Lindsey lowered her voice so the girls all had to lean in—"Johnny Morton bought me a slushie at the game today."

"Who's he?" Ava asked.

"He's on student council," Alex said. "He's in eighth grade and plays baseball and—"

"—is adorably cute," finished Lindsey. "I think it's much cooler to go out with an older boy like Johnny."

"For sure," Emily agreed.

"So you and Corey are totally over?" Alex asked. Ava sensed her sister's disappointment at not being given the chance to fix their broken relationship.

"Totally." Lindsey held out her phone triumphantly. "Johnny just texted me!"

"So there's no reason that we can't talk to Corey and the other guys now?" Ava clarified.

Lindsey shrugged. "I don't care. I can be friends with Corey. Of course, he'll have to hang out with Johnny, too."

Ava shook her head. How could Lindsey

be so sure that she'd soon be going out with Johnny? Ava longed to talk about the game with Corey and Jack. Football was so much simpler.

"How about I invite the guys up to our room?" Ava suggested. "Alex and I are throwing a party!"

"Let's do it," Emily agreed.

"I have lots of soda in my room that I can bring," Rosa offered.

"I have money for snacks." Ava handed Alex a bunch of dollar bills. "Will you get them?" She looked around. The boys had left their post by the reception desk. "I'm going to search for the guys."

Alex made a detour before heading to the vending machines.

"Mom." She tapped her mom's shoulder. "I have a surprise for you!"

Mrs. Sackett turned and chuckled. "First Ava, now you! Did you arrange to buy me a new house to go with the job?"

Alex didn't get the joke. "What job? I got you a dinner reservation."

"Dinner?" Her mom stepped closer to hear her better in the noisy lobby.

"You and Daddy have an eight o'clock reservation tonight at Mercury Grill," Alex said proudly.

"Really?" Mrs. Sackett cried. "I called earlier in the week, but they were booked. How did *you* get us a reservation?"

"I called after the game. I explained that the famous Coach Sackett and his wife wanted to celebrate the big win tonight. And I told them that all the websites and newspapers interviewing Daddy would be interested in printing the name of the restaurant where he chose to eat. Mercury Grill said they have their best table waiting for you," Alex said.

Mrs. Sackett jumped up and down. Alex had never seen her mom do that before. "You are amazing, Alex!"

"Sometimes I am," Alex said. And sometimes she wasn't. She was learning to accept that.

Kind of.

Alex smoothed the dollar bills as she followed signs to the vending machines. She spotted their blue neon glow near the indoor pool. The water shimmered in the dim light. The pool and the surrounding lounge chairs were empty. The moist, chlorine-tinged heat curled the flyaway hairs by her face, and she pushed them back as she scrutinized the choices.

Nacho chips? Vanilla sandwich cookies? M & Ms?

"I always go for the Hershey bar."

The boy's voice startled her. Corey stood alongside the farthest machine. He moved closer.

"What a boring choice," Alex said. "Plain chocolate?"

"It's classic," Corey countered. "Too much stuff in chocolate messes up the taste. Don't tell me you were going for the peanut chews. My grandmother eats those."

"Do not knock peanuts in chocolate! Nothing beats Snickers. Actually, nothing beats a frozen Snickers," Alex replied. She couldn't help grinning at him.

"Frozen candy rules," Corey agreed. "Whoa! You must really be starving. That's a lot of money."

"Everyone's coming up to our room. I'm getting snacks. Didn't Ava tell you?" Alex asked.

"No. I got hungry, so I ditched the guys." He stared at the still pool water for a moment. "What do you mean *everyone*?"

"All the girls, and Ava's getting all the guys to come too," Alex explained.

"Yeah, well, you have fun with that."

"Aren't you coming?" Alex asked.

"Nah. The girls are mad at me 'cause of Lindsey. Aren't you mad too?" he asked.

"I don't care about that. I mean, I do care, because Lindsey's my friend. But I'm not mad at you," Alex said.

"Really? I thought you were."

Alex was surprised that Corey cared what she thought. "Lindsey's not mad anymore either. Everyone's over it."

"Cool." He fiddled with his quarters. He seemed unsure what to do next. He was fidgeting the way he had that time by the stairs at the pizza party.

"You go first. I have to get snacks for everyone, and that's a lot of choosing," she said, stepping aside.

He fed his quarters into the machine. They watched in awkward silence as each clinked down. He pressed D3. "Oh, come on!" he cried, when a pack of Skittles fell in place of his chosen Hershey bar.

Alex couldn't hold back her laughter. "Okay, I have to know. What do you think of Skittles?"

Corey raised his eyebrows. "As a candy? Hate them."

"I knew it!" Alex said triumphantly, thinking back to Lindsey's cake.

"I'm glad you're not mad at me," Corey said.

"For the candy?" Alex asked.

"No. I don't know. For everything." He looked directly at her, and she felt her face grow warm.

"It's hot in here," she mumbled.

"I'm glad you're not mad at me," he repeated.

"You said that already," Alex replied softly.

"Yeah, I guess I did." His deep blue eyes stayed on her.

Does he like me? she wondered. The steam of the indoor pool made it almost impossible to breathe. Impossible to think. She'd liked Corey since the day she'd stepped into Ashland Middle School, but Lindsey was still her friend. Did that matter now that they weren't a couple anymore?

Maybe he doesn't like me, she thought. *Maybe I'm making this all up.*

"Found you, Corey!" Ava's voice rang out. She jogged over to them. "Hey, we're having a party!"

"I heard," Corey said, turning to high-five Ava. "I bet it's no fun up there without me."

"Oh, don't flatter yourself. It's plenty fun," Ava teased.

"Help me choose snacks," Alex said, suddenly

embarrassed by her thoughts. She handed Ava and Corey a few of the dollars. Alex quickly fed her money into the machines, scooping up chips and cookies. She listened to Corey and Ava tease each other, but she didn't look at him. She couldn't. Whatever had just happened had been too weird.

In the elevator, Corey stood beside her. As Ava stepped forward to press the button to their floor, Corey nudged Alex with his elbow, and she turned her head. He silently handed her a Snickers.

Then he smiled.

And Alex knew she wasn't making it up.

Belle Payton isn't a twin herself, but she does have twin brothers! She spent much of her childhood in the bleachers reading—er, cheering them on—at their football games. Though she left the South long ago to become a children's book editor in New York City, Belle still drinks approximately a gallon of sweet tea a week and loves treating her friends to her famous homemade mac-and-cheese. Belle is the author of many books for children and tweens, and is currently having a blast writing two sides to each It Takes Two story.

IT TAKES TWO

More books about Alex and Ava?
That's **TWO** good to be true!

Available at your favorite store!

Did you LOVE reading this book?

Visit the Whyville...

Where you can:

- ○ Discover great books!
- ○ Meet new friends!
- ○ Read exclusive sneak peeks and more!

Log on to visit now!
bookhive.whyville.net